HALF BLOOD

Half Blood

Ilyon Chronicles – Prequel Novella

Jaye L. Knight

Living Sword Publishing
www.livingswordpublishing.com

Half-Blood
Ilyon Chronicles – Prequel Novella

www.ilyonchronicles.com

Published by Living Sword Publishing

Proofread by Kim Huther
www.wordsmithproofreading.com

ISBN-13: 978-0692475416
ISBN-10: 0692475419

To the One who is always calling to us and working
in the midst of our broken lives.

Author's Note

For those of you who have already read some of Jace's story in *Resistance* and the other books of the *Ilyon Chronicles* series, I hope this story satisfies your curiosity and gives you good insight into the past Jace came from and how it has shaped him.

If this is your first experience in the world of Ilyon, you will find a tragic story, but one that ends on a note of hope and points toward God and how He works in even the most broken lives. When everything falls apart and we find ourselves at our lowest, it is in those moments we can find God working and preparing a better future. It is here Jace's story begins, amidst the darkness of cruelty and a fallen world, but it is merely the first step in the man Jace grows to be by the end of the series. I hope you will follow me all the way to that end and see how God can create beauty from ashes.

Principal Cast

Aertus (AYR - tuhs)—Arcacia's male moon god.
Aldor (AL - dohr)—Kalli's husband. An old friend of Rayad.
Aros (AHR - rohs)—Rayad's white horse.
Dane—A cruel man and one of Jace's fellow slaves.
Elôm (EE - lohm)—The one true God of Ilyon.
Jace—A half-ryrik slave.
Jasper—A cruel gladiator owner.
Kalli (KA - lee)—Aldor's wife. An old friend of Rayad.
Niton (NYE - ton)—Rayad's black horse.
Rayad (RAY - ad)—An Arcacian man wanted by the emperor for being a rebel.
Rohir (ROH - heer)—Jace's favorite of Jasper's horses.
Strune—An injured jay that Jace helps.
Vilai (VI - lye)—Arcacia's female moon god.
Zar—Jasper's gladiator trainer and handler.

Ilyon
N
W
E
S
Samara
Amberin
Stonehelm
Sinnai Mts.
Arcacia
Sidian Ocean
Graylin Valley
Dunlow
Valcré
Kinnim
Landale
Ardaluin Bay
Fort Rivor
Mernin
Keaton
Falspar
Troas
Arda

Graer Mts.
Arvael
Trayse River
Bel-gard
Andros Ford
Dorland
Wildmor
Krell Mts.

JACE ROSE UP on his toes and stretched his arm as far as he could; however, though he was taller than the other six-year-olds at the estate, he still couldn't quite reach the top roost in the chicken coop. He puffed out a sigh. It would be so much easier and faster if he could just reach it. In resignation, he grabbed the small stool he kept in the corner and moved it in place. Stepping up onto it, he came face-to-face with one of his master's hens. The hen gave him a wary look, but he'd learned how to handle them. Lightly, he stroked her feathers, calming her. He then slowly reached underneath her warm body for her eggs, and withdrew them before she could peck at his hands.

Once he had checked each hen for eggs, he picked up his full egg basket and left the chicken coop. Cook would be getting impatient by now. He was always in a bad mood in the mornings. Jace set off across the yard toward the kitchen, with quick, but careful, steps. Broken eggs would really make Cook angry.

A horse whinnied and drew Jace's attention to the fields, where most of the slaves worked. He wished he were big enough to work in the fields. It would be better than working around Cook or his wife. They were both mean. If only he could work with the master's horses . . .

Loud, desperate chirping stopped Jace short. His gaze darted to the large willow tree near the master's house, where cruel laughter followed the chirps. Jace's stomach bunched up. A baby bird flapped helplessly on the ground, while Nicolas and Teague, the master's two sons, poked at it with a stick. Jace cast a hesitant look toward the kitchen. Going near the boys would be trouble. It was always better to stay far away from them . . .

The bird chirped pitifully again. Nearby, its mother trilled an alarmed call. Jace breathed in hard and marched toward the boys.

"Leave it alone."

They straightened and spun to face him. Nicolas, the eldest and the one with the stick, drew himself up, though he wasn't any taller than Jace, despite being two years older.

"Look, Teague; the half-blood *slave* just gave us a command."

Jace shrank a little. He shouldn't be speaking to them. "It's just a baby. You . . . you shouldn't hurt it." He gulped as Nicolas took a step closer.

"It's a stupid animal," Nicolas's lip curled, "like you."

Tears rushed up, burning Jace's nose and blurring his eyes. He blinked hard. He wouldn't let Nicolas see him cry. "Please, just leave it alone."

Nicolas let out a harsh laugh and stepped even closer. Jace clutched the full egg basket closer to his stomach, looking toward the kitchen. Could he run?

Nicolas's hands slammed into his shoulders and shoved

him toward the ground. Cold horror flushed through him as he hit the dirt. Something splatted beside him. He held his eyes closed a moment, but then opened them to the terrible sight of cracked shells and oozing egg yolks.

"No," he gasped.

Nicolas and Teague's laughter surrounded him, but he couldn't pull his eyes from the eggs. Cook would be furious! The tears worked their way up again, and one slipped over. He brushed it away, hoping the other boys hadn't noticed.

"Look what you did, half-blood," Nicolas taunted. "You broke all the eggs."

It wasn't my fault. But he was a slave. Slaves didn't get to speak up for themselves, especially not to their masters. He bit his lip to trap his voice inside and hold back the tears.

When Nicolas and Teague finally grew tired of laughing, Nicolas motioned to his brother. "Let's go."

As they passed him, Nicolas kicked Jace hard in the side. He let out a small cry.

"Stupid animal," Nicolas said.

Jace pressed his hand to his throbbing ribs and breathed hard, using his other hand to rub the relentless tears from his eyes. He stared at the eggs again. The urge to run back to the slave quarters and hide in his corner gripped him. But then Cook, or one of the overseers, would come looking for him. It would be even worse then. He had no choice but to face Cook.

Sniffing and blinking rapidly, he picked through the jagged eggshells with dim hope. Maybe there would be enough, and Cook wouldn't notice. When he finished, three unbroken eggs lay inside his basket . . . three left, out of more than a dozen. It would never be enough. Trying to be brave, he pushed to his feet and trudged to the kitchen. At the door, he braced himself before stepping inside.

"Where've you been, boy?" Cook demanded, spotting him immediately. The towering man had his sleeves rolled up to his elbows and a too-small apron tied snug around his large girth. In his hand, he clutched a large wooden spoon that Jace had felt the sting of many times. But it wasn't the spoon that frightened him the most. His gaze shifted to the long switch in the corner.

"I . . ." he gulped.

Cook rounded his large worktable, scattered with ingredients and dishes. His eyes dropped to the egg basket and narrowed. "Where are all the eggs?"

Jace fought to make his tongue work, but lack of moisture made it clumsy. "I fell," he whispered.

"You fell?" Cook repeated coldly.

Jace nodded. Nicolas's laughing face flashed in his mind, but he couldn't place blame on the master's sons. The last time he had been disrespectful of them, Cook had switched him good. He wouldn't risk adding to the beating he already had coming.

Cook jutted his chin toward the door. "Outside."

Jace hunched his shoulders and set the egg basket down. As he turned for the door, he peeked back and caught Cook heading for the switch.

Jace wiped his sleeves across his wet cheeks. He hadn't wanted to cry, but he couldn't help it. At least Nicolas and Teague weren't still around to see him. Amid Cook's grumbling about not having eggs, Jace went on with the rest of his kitchen chores, but the hot, pulsing sting all over his back threatened to call up more tears. He bit his lip to hold back a whimper as he bent down to sweep dirt into a dustpan.

As he worked, the baby bird came to mind. Would it be all right? Would the mother get it back into the nest? Maybe *he* could. He'd climbed the willow tree before, when no one was looking. He was good at it. Glancing at Cook, he swallowed hard. It would be too soon to ask if he could be excused. He would have to wait a bit.

He turned back to his chores. An hour later, he'd finally worked up the courage to approach Cook. The man still grumbled and scowled while he worked, even more than usual. Jace tried to look repentant and uncomfortable, which wasn't at all hard to do. Shifting his weight, he cleared his throat. "Cook, I need to, uh . . . go outside for a minute."

The man glared down at him, and Jace didn't hold eye-contact.

"Fine, but make it quick."

Jace nodded and dashed through the door. Outside, he paused just long enough to make sure the master's sons weren't nearby before he ran toward the willow tree. He just had to find the nest and put the baby bird back before Cook grew suspicious.

His heart thumped as he ran, but, when he reached the tree, it almost stopped. The little bird lay where Nicolas and Teague had left it, but it wasn't moving. Jace dropped to his knees and carefully scooped it into his cupped hands. It flopped over lifelessly in his palms. Streaks of blood matted its feathers from the wounds left by Nicolas's cruel treatment.

Tears gushed into Jace's eyes again. He was too late. He

sniffed, but his cheeks grew warm and wet as he huddled under the tree and cradled the still bird. "I'm sorry I couldn't save you."

He nestled the bird back into the lush grass, where it looked like it was just asleep . . . but it wasn't. It was dead. He sniffed again and rubbed his fists against his eyes. How could anyone be mean enough to kill something?

"Jace!"

Cook's shout sent a jolt through him. Had he been gone that long? He jumped to his feet, swiped away the remaining tears, and bolted back to the kitchen. Cook stood in the doorway, his hands on his hips and a scowl on his face. Pain stabbed Jace's back just thinking about two beatings in one day.

"I'm sorry; I—"

"The master is looking for you," Cook cut in. "You better get yourself up to the front of the house."

Jace stumbled to a halt. He looked toward the front of the house before glancing again at Cook. The master had never summoned him before. Jace had never even seen him up close. Had Nicolas and Teague told their father what he had done? A shiver raced through Jace. What if he was angry? What if he had Jace beaten with one of those leather whips the overseers used on the other slaves, the ones that left awful wounds and made grown men scream?

His legs shook and fear rooted him to the spot.

"Get going, boy!

Cook took a step toward him, and Jace scurried to obey, even though his fear protested every step. Pleas that he could use on his master scrambled around in his mind. He hadn't meant to forget his place and be disrespectful. He'd just wanted to protect the baby bird!

When he reached the front of the manor house, his breath came in short puffs. He stopped and took in the scene. Several other slave children and a few adults stood in a group. A woman's cry drew his gaze to the slaves standing off to the side. Several other women were crying, while their husbands or friends held them back. Jace looked to the grouping of slaves again. They were the children of the crying women.

Something squeezed hard around Jace's stomach. He had seen this happen before. The children were being sold.

A shadow fell over Jace. He flinched and looked up at one of the overseers. The man grabbed him by the arm, dragging him toward the group. "Here he is."

Jace glanced at the coiled whip hanging from the man's belt and didn't try to resist. He caught sight of the master, who only nodded and turned his attention elsewhere. When they reached the group, another man fit a leather collar snugly around his throat. He gasped. He was being sold too!

But he had never been anywhere else! His master's estate was . . . home. No one really liked him, but at least it was familiar. And Cook was mean, but sometimes he did something nice or gave Jace leftovers from the master's meals. What if his new master and fellow slaves were even worse, and never did anything kind? What if they all hated him like Nicolas and Teague did?

He spun around, desperate. There had to be a way he could stay. He would work extra hard, and he would never be disrespectful to Nicolas and Teague again. He would make sure he never broke any more of Cook's eggs, and wouldn't dawdle when he sent him on errands. Straining against the collar, he looked for the master, but he was too far away for Jace to reach.

The truth settled heavily on him. The overseers would take him away from the only place that resembled home and sell him to strangers. He would never see this familiar place again. A lump swelled in his throat.

Tremors gripped him as the overseers guided the group toward a waiting wagon. One by one, they lifted the children into it. Jace was the last. The overseer's strong hands grasped him under the arms and lifted him up with the other children.

In moments, the wagon rolled away from the estate. Jace grasped the side and watched as the manor house shrank away behind them. When it disappeared, he huddled down and hugged his knees to his chest. Several of the other children cried and whimpered for their mothers. He thought of the crying women they had left behind. Would anyone miss him?

No. He was just the half-blood; more of a nuisance than anything. Likely no one would even realize he was gone, except for Cook, but he would just find another slave boy to order around. Jace didn't have a mother or a father to cry over him—not even a memory of them that he could use to pretend.

The ride in the wagon seemed to stretch on for a long time. Jace didn't know how long it was, but his stomach started to pinch with hunger, and his back still hurt as it bumped against the side. He peeked out of the wagon. Only meadows with tall grass surrounded them. In the distance stood a forest, but it was too far away to look like anything more than a dark line. The other children had stopped crying, but a couple of them still sniffled and wiped their faces.

Sometime later, Jace snapped to attention at the sound of voices and commotion. No one else seemed to hear it, until it grew louder and closer. Then the children shifted around, trading wide-eyed looks. A twinge passed through Jace's stomach that wasn't hunger this time.

In another moment, the shadows of buildings blocked the hot sun overhead as they entered a city. Jace got to his knees and looked over the side of the wagon, his eyes widening. He had never seen a city before. There were so many people! A group of laughing children raced by, a dog bounding after them. What was it like to be free and play like that? Cook hardly ever let him play, and none of the other children wanted to play with him anyway.

He sighed and sank back in the wagon bed. He didn't want to see any more of the city.

Shouts drifted from somewhere ahead, growing steadily louder. Jace didn't pay much attention to them until the wagon stopped. The overseers came around to the back, and a couple of the youngest children whimpered as they reached for them.

One at a time, the men pulled the children out, attaching their collars to one long rope. When the wagon was empty, one of the overseers tugged on the rope, and they all moved in the direction of the shouting. Jace looked ahead, but he couldn't make out much through the large crowd. His insides shrank. He didn't like so many people.

On the opposite side of the crowd, a platform caught Jace's eye. Around it stood groups of people, either tied or chained up just like him. The shouting man stood upon the platform, motioning at another large, shirtless man with a metal collar around his neck. Now it was clear. The man was calling out prices. Jace swallowed hard. He had overheard some of the older slaves back at his master's estate talk about slave auctions before, but he'd never thought he would be in one.

Tremors rippled through him again, but, as time dragged on, with one slave sold after another, he grew more tired than scared. And he was hungry. His stomach kept gurgling, and his legs hurt. He'd never gone so long without food before. He glanced at the master's overseers, but didn't dare ask to sit down, far too afraid that one of them might decide to use their whip.

Sweat built up under his collar and rolled down his back. He squirmed. The sun was so hot. In front of him, a couple of children swayed. He blinked his gritty eyes and watched, almost mesmerized, as one of the little girls fell down.

"Get up." The overseer jabbed her leg with his boot.

She yelped and scrambled to her feet. Jace blinked hard and shook his head, determined to remain standing.

After what felt like hours and hours, the overseer tugged on the rope, guiding them forward. That's when it started. The older, more valuable slaves were sold first—people in the still-thick crowd calling out their bids—and then came the children. As each child was sold and led away in tears, Jace's heart beat harder, echoing loudly in his ears. Two children left. He peered through the crowd in the direction of the wagon. Could he somehow get free and run to it? Maybe he could hide underneath and get back to the estate so he could beg Cook to ask the master to keep him. He didn't want to go anywhere else. His tears blurred the crowd. He shook all over, cold covering him.

His collar jerked against his throat.

"Move," the overseer's rough voice snapped.

It was happening.

He stumbled forward and stopped at the steps up to the platform. The auctioneer at the top waited for him, but Jace couldn't move. His body didn't want to work, but then hands gripped him under the arms and hauled him up onto the platform. The auctioneer took the rope attached to his collar and led him to the edge of the platform, where everyone could see him.

"Here, now, we have a strong young lad. He'll grow into a good worker for your fields."

Jace looked down at the crowd pressed close to the platform for a good view of him. None of them had kind faces. He trembled. *Please don't want me.* If no one bought him, the overseers would have to take him back to the estate, wouldn't they?

He dropped his gaze to his dirty bare feet. He didn't like people staring at him.

From somewhere in the crowd came a gasp, and exclamations followed.

"Look at his ears!"

"What is he?"

Jace reached for his ears, his fingers touching the point at the top. No one else had pointed ears. It was a ryrik thing. He didn't really know much about ryriks. All the other slaves said they were monsters who liked to hurt people—no better than wild animals. He tried to brush his hair down over his ears, but it wasn't long enough. Sometimes the other children teased him about his ears, but he hadn't realized they were so strange.

He peeked at the people again, and his face grew hot. Everyone in the crowd gave him odd looks—kind of like the other children always gave him if he asked to play with them.

Why were they so afraid? He wasn't a ryrik, at least not completely. He would never hurt anyone, not even Nicolas and Teague.

Then, amidst the murmuring, a man called out, "Is he a ryrik?"

"Half ryrik," the auctioneer answered.

The murmuring grew. Though some weren't more than whispers, the words reached Jace's ears—*dangerous, monster, animal, soulless*. He tried to back away from their accusing eyes, but the collar pulled hard against his throat and held him in place. Did they really think he was dangerous? A monster? Such words and worse continued to rise from the crowd, and Jace struggled to breathe against the growing pressure in his chest. The other slaves avoided him, and Nicolas and Teague sometimes said mean things, but not like this. Would everyone outside of the estate hate him this much?

Another man's voice rose up from the crowd to Jace's right. "How old is he?"

The other people hushed and, for a moment, all was silent. The auctioneer nudged Jace. "How old are you, boy?"

Jace opened his mouth, but his voice stuck in his throat. "Six," he managed in a whisper. At least, that's what Cook told him. No one really knew when he was born.

"He's six years old," the auctioneer announced. "He's already tall. Imagine how strong he'll be at twelve or sixteen."

"And dangerous!" a woman cried out. "I wouldn't let him anywhere near my young ones."

Several others voiced their agreement.

Jace gulped. *I'm not dangerous.*

Then the man who had asked his age spoke again. "I'll pay two hundred for him."

No one in the crowd spoke up with a better offer. For that silent minute, Jace studied what he could see of the man. He was wealthy—one of the best-dressed men in the crowd—but the size of his arms and shoulders didn't give him the appearance of a gentleman like Jace's old master. His hard, angular face and dark eyes put a rock in Jace's middle. Instinctively, he knew this was not a good man. He silently begged someone else in the crowd to bid on him, but not a single person spoke.

When the auctioneer called out "Sold", Jace's eyes filled with burning moisture. He fought mightily to hold the tears back. If his new master saw him crying or thought him weak, it might just make things worse. The man stomped up to the platform, handed over the money, and took the rope of Jace's collar. Without a word, he marched to the steps. Jace had to jog to keep up with him and avoid being strangled. Just before he left the platform, he looked back desperately for his old master's overseers. Maybe they would change their minds. However, they were already leading the next child up to the platform and didn't even spare him a glance.

Nine Years Later

JACE STEPPED THROUGH the gates of the fenced-in slave yard and cast a wary look around. Of the seven estates he had belonged to since he was first sold as a young boy, this appeared to be one of the worst as far as living conditions went. The cramped, dirty area and barn-like housing sheds gave the appearance of a cattle yard. Apparently, that was what his newest master saw them as—beasts of burden.

He trailed after his master's overseer and the three other new slaves. As they passed by those who were already present, Jace noted their drawn and smudged faces. Most gave him no more than a disinterested glance, but suspicion bloomed in the eyes of some. By the end of the night, everyone would know of his mixed blood. Such news always traveled fast, along with fear and revulsion.

In the center of the yard, the overseer stopped and turned to remove the collars from Jace and the other slaves' throats. He then left them without a word. Two of the new slaves glanced at each other with looks of fear and uncertainty.

They weren't much older than Jace. This was probably the first time they had found themselves sold. No master ever cared if a slave considered a certain estate home. They were simply commodities to be bought and sold at the whim of whomever fate decided was above them.

Jace crossed the yard to the farthest corner, away from everyone, and sat down to observe. It was always best to learn right away who to avoid and who posed the greatest threats. Early on, he had tried to get to know people and even make friends, but the moment they learned of his ryrik blood, they would shy away from him. He didn't even try now. It wasn't worth the effort or pain of false hope. People couldn't be trusted to see him as anything more than an animal—a monster of revolting origin.

For half an hour, he sat and watched. During that time, more and more of the slaves cast shadowed glances his way. Like a devouring fire, word spread. No doubt the three young men he had arrived with had set the first flames. It appeared that their sharing of such information helped bond them to the group, as if in doing so they had saved their fellow slaves from danger. Jace couldn't really blame them for doing whatever they could to establish their position in this new place.

When twilight fell a short time later, a bell rang out. The slaves grouped together and formed a line at the gates. Jace rose and approached the end of it. This must be how they received their supper. The line crept forward. Finally, Jace reached the small opening in the fence, where a grumpy-faced man, who reminded him of the old cook he used to work for, handed him a wooden bowl of unappetizing mash and a rock-like biscuit.

Jace took it and turned to peer around the yard. The other slaves had lit small fires here and there, and sat huddled around them. The early spring air was indeed chilly. He cautiously approached one of the fires to gain a little warmth, though he kept enough distance from the other slaves. They each gave him guarded looks, as one might give a scavenging dog that stayed nearby but was never fully tamed.

Sitting in the dirt, he looked down into his bowl, and his stomach recoiled. The mash only seemed fit for a stray dog. He couldn't tell what it consisted of, but it resembled the slop he used to feed his last master's pigs. At least it didn't smell as bad. He tested a small bite. Though bland and mealy, it wasn't as hard to swallow as he'd expected. The biscuit, on the other hand, was like chewing dirt. The man at the fence certainly wasn't much of a cook. Jace could probably bake better biscuits.

He was about to help the dry mouthful down with another bite of mash when a group of five men caught his attention. They were big, and carried themselves with a dangerous air of self-importance. The other slaves seemed to shrink in their presence. When they reached the fire, the man at the head of the group towered over a thin young woman, who appeared to be blind in one eye. She cowered and sat stone-still. The man bent over her.

"You're not gonna try to resist now, are you?"

The girl's lip trembled, and she shook her head. Her voice barely squeaked out, "No, Dane."

She handed over her biscuit and spooned almost half of her mash into Dane's bowl. Jace's grip tightened around his own bowl as he glared at the cruel brute. Dane and the other men worked their way around the fire, doing the same with each of the slaves. No wonder they were all so thin. It was an obvious routine among them, and not one resisted.

When Dane approached Jace, he pushed to his feet, defiance creeping up inside of him. He almost matched the man in height, though Dane's bulk was double his own. Dane looked him up and down, hints of a sneer on his face.

"So you're the half-blood."

Jace raised his chin. He would not cower or give in to intimidation. Men like this always preyed on such weakness.

Dane's brows shifted upward. "You like trouble, half-blood?"

Jace maintained firm eye-contact. "No."

"Then here's how things work around here. You hand over half your rations, and there won't be any trouble."

Jace glanced at the men behind Dane. Their threatening looks warned him to do as Dane commanded. Once he backed down, though, it would establish Dane as the superior man, and give him full control over Jace.

"No."

Dane's brows rose even higher as everything around them grew unnaturally quiet. Every eye in the yard fixed on them. A worming of fear twisted through Jace, but he forced it away. He would not fear these men. Fear was their tool of control.

For a moment, it appeared Dane might leave him alone, but then the back of his hand slammed across Jace's jaw. He stumbled, and the bowl fell from his hand. Before he could recover from the shock, Dane's fist hammered into the side of his head and sent him to the ground. He scrambled to regain his feet, his insides screaming in warning at his vulnerable position, but a breath-snatching kick to his ribs sent him back to the dirt. Still, he fought to get up. He lunged for Dane's legs, but the man caught him in the chin with his knee, and Jace fell hard, his vision blurring. Another kick to the side ripped a groan from his chest.

Dane stood over him and growled, "I don't know what it was like where you came from, half-blood, but around here you do exactly as I say."

He gave Jace a final, hard kick that held a warning. Jace gasped and grabbed his side as Dane and the other men strode away, a couple of them laughing. He lay on his back for a long moment, trying to catch his breath. His ribs ached and his chin throbbed. Gingerly, he touched the stinging area on the side of his jaw. His fingers came away coated in blood. Still holding his chest, he slowly pushed himself up. His head pounded. He looked at his spilled supper spattering the ground, and then across the yard to where Dane and his men enjoyed their meals. He clenched his jaw and glared at Dane. The man might have won tonight, but Jace had no intention of letting that be the end of it.

The blistering heat of summer burned down on Jace's back as he swung the scythe through the grass. Sweat rolled down his face and stung his eyes, but he kept moving forward. The overseers were always watching and quick to get after anyone who lagged. The last couple of months had been the hardest he had faced as far as labor. His previous masters had never put him to work in the fields full-time. The back-breaking work left him barely able to stand some days, especially with such meager meals, but it did have its advantages. Since arriving, his muscle mass had almost doubled with the work.

He had never been so strong in his life, and strength was just what he needed.

He sent a glare at Dane, who worked across the field. Every night when Dane took his food or hit him to remind him of his place, Jace accepted it quietly, but he wouldn't put up with it forever. If no one else would do something about Dane's treatment of the weakest slaves, then Jace would. He'd had enough with being kicked around and watching others suffer. Just last month, the master had ordered Nettie, the girl with the blind eye, to be whipped for not doing her work to his satisfaction. Had he even known that her struggle came from hunger, since Dane took so much of her food? Would he have cared?

She died a few days later. Her malnourished body couldn't handle the whipping.

It was all Jace could do not to confront Dane that very night, but he had forced himself to bide his time and grow a bit stronger. Now he felt ready. Although he couldn't do anything about his master's cruelty, he could do something about Dane. The man had terrorized them all for long enough. Jace intended to put a stop to it, whether that meant simply beating Dane in a fight and establishing dominance, or . . .

He buried the rest of that thought. All he knew was that he was done being the man's victim. He would stand up to him again, come what may.

Jace's anger rested like a hot ember inside him and fueled his determination. Focusing on his plans helped him push through the exhaustion of the afternoon until, at last, all the slaves filed back to the yard for the night. The sun had sunk by now, shadowing the area in twilight. Inside the yard, he waited for his turn to get water from the small well. Once he had quenched his thirst, he stepped back and looked around for Dane. He and his cohorts stood near the wall, waiting for their supper rations. Jace narrowed his eyes. It would be the last time the man put himself before others.

He waited at the back of the supper line, his stomach cramping for reasons other than hunger. When he received his bowl, he could tell it was the last remnants of the mash pot, but tonight it wouldn't matter. He scanned the yard. Dane and the others were already making their rounds. Drawing a breath, Jace set out for his usual spot near the farthest fire, where the outcast slaves congregated. Yet even here he found no camaraderie. He was just too different; below even the lowest of them.

He sat down and waited until Dane made his way toward the fire. After robbing the others, he approached Jace last, a smirk twisting his lips. He seemed to take the most pleasure in tormenting Jace. But not for much longer.

Jace pushed to his feet and met Dane's gaze with an openly-defiant look.

Dane's eyes narrowed as they came face to face. "Hand over your rations, half-blood."

"No."

Anger hardened Dane's features. "You give me what's mine, or I'll beat you senseless and leave you with nothing."

Jace hesitated. He had this one chance to back out; perhaps even avoiding a beating. Uncertainty ghosted through his mind. He had been in a few scuffles, but had never fought anyone like Dane before. Did he even stand a chance? The smoldering anger resurfaced and chased away the doubt. If he didn't stand up to Dane now, the cruelty would continue. For once, he wanted to take control of his own life.

Jace pulled his shoulders back. "You can try."

Dane stiffened. He handed his bowl to his friends, and Jace quickly set his own down. There was no going back now. The only question was whether he would win or would spend the next couple of weeks healing from what would surely be a severe beating if Dane came out the victor. Jace didn't care. Not anymore.

He barely had time to straighten before Dane lunged at him with his fist, but he'd anticipated such a move. Dodging the blow, he threw his own attack, his curled fist sinking into Dane's stomach. Satisfaction flushed through him as the man doubled over with a gasp. It was about time he tasted a little of the abuse he always doled out.

The gratification died quickly as Dane came back with a shattering blow to Jace's chin. Light flashed in his vision, and his knees almost buckled. He stumbled away from Dane, trying to clear his head. The ground shifted beneath his feet. Heavy steps pursued him. He turned and barely avoided an uppercut to the chin that would have landed him on his back. Throwing out his fist, he caught Dane in the ribs, but not with enough force or accuracy to do any real damage. Not like Dane's answering maul-like blow to Jace's gut.

His legs wobbled again. The air rushed from his lungs, and he struggled to draw more. He scrambled away from Dane, desperately gulping for air. Panic flitted through his jumbled thoughts. He was going to lose this fight.

Dane came up behind him. "You'll be sorry you ever chose to defy me, half-blood."

In that split-second moment, Jace imagined himself lying in a battered, bleeding heap once Dane was through, and the fight hardened inside of him. If Dane did succeed in beating him senseless, then at least Jace would make him work for it.

With a shout, he spun around and drove his fist straight into Dane's nose. The man's hands flew to his face and, this time, he was the one who stumbled. Jace stalked after him. Dane lowered his hands to prepare for an attack, and blood streamed bright red from his nose. Even so, fury lit his eyes. He came at Jace in a rage.

Blow after blow they traded. Dane's fists found their targets more often, but Jace continued to press forward. He would not back down. Not until his body could no longer move.

Though he had avoided previous attempts, one of Dane's uppercuts finally caught Jace in the chin. It wasn't as powerful as it could have been, but it still threw him off-balance. He hit the ground hard. He tried to roll and regain his feet, but Dane was on top of him in a second.

Fingers closed around Jace's throat and squeezed. Jace choked, unable to draw any air into his lungs. He grabbed Dane's wrists and fought to pry his hands away. When they wouldn't budge, he clawed at the man's bloodied face, but Dane twisted away and out of reach. His heart hammered his ribs with shattering force. He needed air. Just as the panic ignited full-force, searing heat burst from his heart and raced through his nerves and veins, setting his blood on fire and surging through his whole body. Every sense sharpened, and strength poured into his muscles. He slammed his fists against the joints in Dane's arms. The man's hold loosened. Jace sucked in a great gulp of air and threw Dane off of him.

He jumped to his feet, that fiery heat still coursing through him, and lunged at Dane, who had yet to rise. Jace wrapped his arms around the man's neck. Dane struggled to shrug him off, but Jace held fast. Then, with a burst of raw energy, Jace twisted his arms.

Dane fell limp at his feet.

Jace waited a moment for him to rise, ready to knock him back down and claim victory. But he didn't. He just lay there, completely still. Not even his chest rose with the panting breaths he had breathed only moments ago. A jolt of ice streaked through the fire inside Jace.

Dane was dead.

He had killed him.

He took a shaky step back. *What have I done?* He looked at his hands, and then at the crowd that had gathered to watch. All were silent, but, when his gaze met them, many of the women gasped, and the entire group took a step away from him. From somewhere came the frightened murmur, "Look at his eyes! They're glowing!"

A palpable fear radiated from the group as they all stared at him as if he were a feral animal about to attack them. He shook his head, and his gaze fell again on Dane's lifeless body. His chest seized up. With his own hands, he had taken a life. *No.* He shook his head again. Such a thing could *never* be undone.

He was a murderer.

The gate across the yard opened. The master and several of his overseers marched in.

"What is going on here?"

Everyone shrank even farther away from Jace, leaving him alone in his condemning position—standing over the body of a dead man. A man *he* had killed.

A haze engulfed Jace, quieting everything around him except for the powerful thudding of his heart and the crushing truth of what he had done. He would die for this. He *deserved* to die for this.

Hands seized him and dragged him forward. The haze broke as he met his master's accusing eyes. Jace had no excuses for what he had done. He had wanted to stop Dane's cruelty, but that could never absolve him of the guilt that now hung on him like an enormous weight.

Movement drew his attention to his master's head overseer. The large, scar-faced man had just pulled his long leather whip from his belt. The heat still stirring within Jace died to a bone-numbing cold. He didn't fear much anymore, but those whips . . . Time and again he had seen how they stripped even the most hardened men of their strength. He had done everything possible over the years to avoid them, but that had finally ended. Now he deserved every lash he received.

The other overseers yanked off his shirt, shoving him up to the post in one corner of the yard, and chained his arms around it. He drew a shaky breath, unsure of what would be more painful in the coming hours—the whip, or the unrelenting guilt that tore through his mind with the same ferocity with which the whip would tear at his back.

JACE RAISED HIS head out of the dirt, but the motion set fire to his back like a thousand razor-tipped claws ripping into his flesh. He let it fall again. There was nothing to see in the small, windowless confinement cell anyway. Only dirt and musty straw—the perfect conditions to breed infection in the open wounds across his back. If that didn't kill him, the sweltering heat would. The sun beating down turned the enclosed cell into a sweltering oven. He could never tell if the moisture rolling along his skin was sweat or blood. He tried to swallow, but his throat was as dry as the dust against his cheek. He hadn't had any water since before they had thrown him in here after the whipping last night . . . or was it two days ago? Three? He didn't know, and he didn't care; just so long as he died soon. Then the pain would end—from both his wounds and his memories.

He squeezed his eyes shut, fighting to keep the images out. Yes, it was true, deep down he had wanted Dane dead, but he hadn't been prepared for how it would feel to go through with it—how it would torment him afterward. He hadn't been prepared for that burning heat that had taken hold of him, proving beyond all doubt what he was.

A monster—just like they all said.

The memories of that fiery heat wouldn't let him go. He hadn't experienced it before. Never had his ryrik blood been more obvious than in those moments it had set fire to his heart, filling him with strength he had never known he possessed—strength to overcome . . . to kill.

His eyes burned, and he squeezed them more tightly against the gathering moisture. Clenching his fist, he hit the ground weakly, and barely stifled a groan at the fresh wave of pain it brought. Why hadn't his master just killed him? Why? A small cry forced past his cracked lips, and he begged the answering silence for death.

The grating shriek of the bolt on the door dragged Jace into an unwelcome consciousness. He was still alive. He let out a hard breath and would have shouted in frustration had his throat not been so dry and raw. Why did his body cling so stubbornly to life? Another curse of his ryrik blood. It was too resilient—too determined to fight.

Light poured into the cell. Jace squinted, but couldn't lift his head to see who approached. Had he anyone to pray to, he would have prayed for a sword through the heart. Instead, a strong hand gripped his wrist and attached rough metal before grabbing his other and pulling them behind his back. The wounds on his shoulders tore open afresh and ripped a cry from his throat. He bit down on the groan that followed as the man hauled him up. His legs struggled to support him, and the spinning sensation in his head tipped him toward the far wall. He blinked hard to clear his vision and managed to keep his feet.

The man guided him out of the cell. Sunlight almost blinded Jace but, after a moment, he made out his master's form. The man stood incredibly straight, as if attached to a pole, and peered at Jace with a level of disgust that again begged the question—why had he not just killed him?

Jace stumbled to a halt in front of his master, but couldn't hold his critical gaze. The man was upstanding, civilized . . . human.

Jace's attention strayed to the other man at his master's side—a stranger. He was shorter, broad-shouldered, but on the heavy side. The fabric of his oddly purple doublet stretched taut around the buttons along his middle. Behind him stood a massive bear of a man. He crossed his thick forearms and peered at Jace with a hard look.

The man in purple stepped forward and looked Jace up and down with squinty eyes the color of a mud puddle. He circled Jace, examining him from every angle, as one might inspect a horse or cattle. Jace struggled not to sway, his head still spinning. It was hard to stand straight with the constant pulsating pain in his back.

"How old is he?" the man asked from behind him.

"Fifteen, about," his master answered. "We're not sure exactly when or even how he was born. He's no doubt the spawn of unspeakable evil against some poor woman."

Jace grimaced at the sting of those words. Sometimes he wished he knew where he came from, but his master was right. He was the product of a depraved man's violent and vile act. It was the only plausible explanation for his existence.

And now it was clear that the same violence ran in his own abhorrent mixed blood.

"He's quite muscular and tall for fifteen." The man in purple came to stand in front of him again and squeezed first his arm and then his shoulder.

Jace sucked in his breath when the man's fingertips dug into a wound.

"That's his ryrik blood. He's more ryrik than human, I say. Behaves and looks like one. You should have seen the look in his eyes the other night. He's a killer."

The man in purple turned to Jace's master. "He snapped the man's neck, you say?"

A vise closed around Jace's heart with the reminder of what he'd done. A desperate cry rose within him to respond that he hadn't meant to . . . but hadn't he? Hadn't it been in him all this time, deep down, to stop Dane for good? He *was* a killer. A wretched, worthless creature. Tears bit his eyes. His knees wobbled in his desire to fall at his master's feet and beg the man to put him out of his misery. However, a flame of defiance grew inside his chest at the idea of such weakness.

Jace's master nodded, spearing him with a look of both hatred and fear. "He's a danger to society. He should be put down."

Yes. Please. Do it. Jace's heart pounded with the silent plea.

"Well, fortunately for you, I make my living on dangerous men. How much did you pay for him?"

The way the man in purple peered at Jace formed a lump in his already-swollen throat. Greediness filled the man's eyes. He cared only for profit, and Jace had a feeling his life was about to become an even darker pit than it was already. But, after eight different masters, how could he expect anything more?

"Three hundred. I thought he'd be good in the fields with his size, but I should have known better than to take a risk on such an animal."

Jace winced. How many times had men called him that? Dozens, hundreds of times? Yet it never hurt any less.

"I'll give you fifty for him."

It was hardly the price of a goat.

Jace's master scoffed. "I won't take any less than two hundred."

"He's wounded. How am I to know if he'll even heal properly? He could very well die of infection, not to mention the resources it'll take to tend to him."

The master narrowed his eyes, and Jace looked between the two men. Did they ever consider how it felt to be discussed and haggled over, as if he were nothing more than an object? No. He was just an animal to them.

"Fine," his master conceded, "I'll take one hundred for him."

The man in purple gave the offer a long moment of consideration, but that greedy look in his eyes told Jace what his answer would be.

"Deal." The man drew a leather pouch from his belt and counted out a handful of gold coins. He handed them over and, once again, Jace was sold as livestock. Gesturing to the hulk behind him, the man in purple ordered, "Zar, see to him."

Zar grunted and took a length of chain and a metal collar from his own thick belt, attaching it around Jace's neck. Jace swallowed against the cool metal. The sensation sent a sinking feeling through his stomach, but a spark of fight ignited with it. He didn't want to have anything to do with whatever this man planned for him. No normal person would have taken him after what he had done, but Jace was in no condition to fight anyone.

Zar tugged the chain, and the two of them trailed after Jace's new master. As they passed through the yard, Jace glanced at a few of the other slaves, who had paused to watch. At their fearful, mistrusting expressions, he turned away and hunched his shoulders. It didn't matter that, in killing Dane, he had actually done them a favor. They would only remember him as a monster . . . a murderer.

He didn't look back when they left the large estate, but he did lift his head to see the city about a mile up the road. By the time they reached it, he struggled to keep up with the pace. His head beat like the inside of a drum from lack of water, and his back was screaming. A haze blurred his vision, and he blinked to clear it, but it lingered at the edges. Zar tugged on the chain when he slowed, and he almost tripped.

Near the center of the city, they arrived at a grand townhouse, but they bypassed the front entrance and came to a large stone wall that stretched out behind the building. Jace's new master drew a key from his pocket and unlocked a tall, arched gate. Inside, Jace found an enormous courtyard portioned off from the house itself by iron bars.

Over a dozen brawny, fierce-looking men occupied a large sandy area in one corner. Most were paired off and faced each other with a variety of weapons—some real and others of wood. Metal rang out amongst grunts, curses, and a sudden bark of deep laughter. Jace didn't have much time to dwell on the men. Zar led him into a small outbuilding along the wall that housed a few cots, benches, and shelves containing an array of what appeared to be medical supplies. Here, Zar unchained his wrists and removed the collar from his throat. He then handed him a bulging waterskin.

"Drink," he ordered in a deep, growling voice.

Jace needed no prompting. He raised the waterskin to his lips and drank until he had to pause for breath. His headache began to lessen, and a little more strength flowed into his body. Now his eyes locked with the man in purple, who stepped forward.

"I'm Jasper, your new master."

Jace gave him wary look. "What do you want with me?"

The man gripped his belt and pulled his shoulders back in self-importance. "I'm not quite sure yet, but no one's ever heard of a half-ryrik before. That makes you a spectacle, and people are always willing to pay for a good spectacle."

Jace's insides tensed up, and he crushed his teeth together. A spectacle. Would Jasper parade him around for people to stare at with disdain and fear? An instinct to escape gripped him, setting his nerves to burning with the urge to flee. Zar blocked the door, as if he knew exactly what was going through Jace's mind. Their eyes locked for a brief moment, and in them Jace saw not only a challenge, but also an immovable determination to keep him where he was.

"First, however, we must make sure you don't die of infection and waste my money."

Jace's attention snapped back to Jasper, who approached one of the medical cabinets. Jace flinched when Zar took him by the arm and pushed him toward one of the cots.

"Lie down."

Jace glanced from him to Jasper, and then to the cot. The way his back burned now, cleaning and dressing it would surely be agony. He would rather they leave him to die of infection. But what choice did he have? Hating both Zar and his new master, Jace eased stomach-down onto the cot, biting his lip to stop a groan. Zar leaned over him and held his arms down as Jasper approached. A jolt of panic clawed its way through Jace at what was to come and ignited that same warmth in his blood he had experienced a couple of days ago. He breathed hard and clutched the sides of the cot.

Cool liquid splashed onto his back, but immediately turned to fire, searing through his nerves. A cry he could barely restrain jumped to his throat. Pungent alcohol reached his nose as more liquid hit his back, followed by a rough cloth. Jasper dragged it along the wounds. Jace's jaw almost cracked as he ground his teeth together. The pain overwhelmed him, engulfing his back as if from a hundred branding irons. He fought desperately for strength to endure, but couldn't contain the cry any longer. It ripped past his throat, and he tried to get away from Jasper's rough treatment, but Zar was too strong. The pain intensified mercilessly until, at last, a painless black void overtook him.

A ROOSTER CROWED, breaking the stillness of dawn with its harsh, shrieking call that sounded as though someone had once tried to wring its neck. Jace was tempted to wring it himself after waking to such a jarring and unpleasant sound for over a month. He rubbed his hands over his face and sat up on the thin straw pallet in his cell. To his left and across from him, the rest of Jasper's gladiators stirred in their own cells, grumbling, cursing, and muttering threats against the bird as well. He had to wonder if Jasper had deliberately purchased the most annoying rooster in the entire city.

A door opened, and Zar entered the cellblock that lay under Jasper's house. One by one, he opened the cells to let the men out. Jace rose and stretched his muscles. A twinge passed through his back that was still tender at times, and the healing scars pulled. Those first several days had been pure agony, but he had survived it, unfortunately.

Zar reached his cell last and pulled the door open. They said nothing as Jace stepped out and trailed after the other men. In the courtyard, the gladiators stood around a large washbasin, talking and insulting each other. Jace did not join them. He could get his own bucket of water from the well. As he passed by, one of the brutish fighters called out, "Better get to work, stable boy!"

The rest of them laughed, but Jace kept his gaze ahead. It was either "stable boy" or "half-blood". He didn't think anyone but Jasper and Zar actually knew his name. Leaving their laughter and crude talk behind, he entered the stable where six of Jasper's horses resided. The smell of the animals wrapped around him with a comfort that was the only thing he looked forward to every morning. He didn't mind doing the job of a stable boy. In fact, he enjoyed it. Horses had always had a special appeal to him. His sixth master had used him to break horses, putting him on the most dangerous and stubborn ones. He was, after all, expendable; yet to work with the powerful animals was one of the rare high points of Jace's life.

One of Jasper's riding geldings, a large bay, stuck his head over the stall door and nickered quietly. The smallest smile tugged at Jace's lips. The horse was his personal favorite. He walked to the stall and rubbed the soft area on the horse's neck just behind his ear.

"Hey, Rohir."

If only people were more like horses—accepting, trusting.

The gelding nosed his chin and then nibbled on his shirt, looking for a treat. Jace glanced to the door and pulled a small piece of bread he had saved from his supper out of his pocket. Rohir's lips and warm breath tickled his palm as he took the bread from his hand.

"Good boy."

A couple of the other horses looked out from their stalls to see if they would get any treats, too, but if Jace saved enough for all of them, he would lose half his supper. Walking to the corner, he picked up an armful of sweet-smelling hay and brought it to Rohir's stall. While the horse munched contently, he fed the rest of the waiting animals before grabbing a pitchfork to clean up after them. As he worked on the second-to-last stall, Zar's gravelly voice came from outside.

"Half-blood!"

Jace sighed. Even if the man knew his name, he never used it. He laid the pitchfork aside and walked toward the door, but his feet dragged. Why would Zar take him away from his work? For his first few weeks here, Jasper had assigned him to working in the stable, cleaning and repairing the gladiators' weapons and armor, and other menial labor. Deep down, he hoped it would stay this way. He didn't mind it as long as he was left alone. However, a pinching in his stomach told him things were about to change again.

He stepped out into the courtyard. The first bit of sunlight was warming the stones. To his right, commotion came from the mess hall where the other men ate their breakfast. Usually Jace showed up once they were finished and took whatever was left. His attention fixed on Zar.

"Go eat your breakfast," the man jabbed his thumb toward the mess hall, "and be quick about it. The master wants you."

Jace glanced back at the stable, but he had no desire to find out what disobedience would cost. He trudged across the courtyard and warily entered the mess hall. A few of the men cast a hostile glance his way, but most continued with their boisterous exchanges and ignored him. He walked to the kitchen area, where the grubby cook ladled out a bowl of bland porridge for him. The man offered a hard roll as well, but Jace turned it down. Wondering what Jasper could want with him didn't leave him with much of an appetite.

He shoveled the porridge into his mouth and swallowed it down, heeding Zar's warning. From his observations since arriving here, Jasper was often short on patience. He handed the bowl back to the cook a couple of minutes later and hurried outside. Zar waited for him near one of the supply sheds. As Jace crossed the courtyard, Zar picked up a chain and metal collar. Jace swallowed hard. Not many things were more demeaning than being led around like a dog on a leash.

"Come."

Zar entered the shed, and Jace followed. Just inside, they met Jasper. He tossed a cloth bundle at Jace.

"Change into this."

Jace held it up to find a dark-gray sleeveless tunic that was tattered and fraying around the edges. Slowly, he pulled his own shirt off and slipped the tunic on. From a nearby bench, Jasper grabbed a scuffed and worn black leather jerkin and handed it to Jace next. "Now this."

Jace eyed it a moment, his unease growing, but he obeyed.

"Good; now tie your hair back."

Jace stiffened as Jasper tried to hand him a leather tie. He had let his black hair grow long for a purpose: to hide the one most noticeable aspect of his ryrik blood—his pointed ears.

Jasper's face grew hard. "Do it or I'll just cut if off."

Jace ground his teeth together and tied his hair back, giving full view of his ears. Jasper looked him over and nodded with the sickening grin he wore whenever he was thinking about how something could profit him.

"Excellent. Now you look appropriately fierce."

Jace narrowed his eyes. "For what?"

"You'll see." Jasper snapped his fingers at Zar. "Let's be off. We don't want to miss the morning crowd."

Mention of a crowd tied Jace's stomach in a knot. He forcibly had to stop himself from resisting Zar when the man locked the collar around his throat. His feet dragged, passing through the courtyard to the gate, but Zar gave the chain a sharp tug to hurry him up. Outside, two of Jasper's house slaves waited, balancing long poles and a roll of bright red fabric on their shoulders. Jasper took the lead, and the five of them marched into the city.

Jace had not been outside his master's residence since he first arrived just over a month ago. The city buzzed with commotion, and, with each new person they passed, his discomfort grew. He hung his head and tried not to meet anyone's gaze. Without being able to hide his ears, he felt exposed. One curious glance would make it clear to anyone what he was. Luckily, most were in too big a hurry to notice him, though he had a feeling that wouldn't last long.

The hum of conversation grew ahead of them, and Jace looked up. The number of people more than doubled as they neared the center of the city. When he caught sight of brightly-colored awnings and stalls, his heart tripped. A market. Memories of standing on the auction block for the first time several years ago wormed in. The terror of it still had the power to rob him of breath. He slowed again, but the metal collar dug into his neck.

"Move, boy," Zar grumbled.

Jace tried to shake off the cold in his blood as they entered the marketplace. They zigzagged through the milling crowd, until they reached an open spot on the far side. Jasper snapped his fingers at the two slaves. "Set up here."

The two of them jumped to work putting up the red awning, and Jasper took two metal stakes and a hammer from the satchel one of them had carried. With the sharp ringing of metal against metal, he drove the stakes into the ground about five feet apart. He then pulled two chains out of the satchel and turned to Jace.

"Time to see if you are worth the time and effort."

He handed the chains to Zar, who attached them to Jace's wrists and then to the stakes, leaving him to stand between them. There wasn't much slack in the chain—just enough to reach up to his head. He glared suspiciously at Jasper, but the man now faced the crowded market square. He spread his arms wide to gain their attention, though his garish bright-red doublet would have had no trouble doing that on its own.

"Ladies and gentlemen, step forward to see a most unusual spectacle. I give you a captive ryrik!" He gestured to Jace. A few women nearby touched their chests and took a step back, but he had succeeded in gaining attention. "And, men, for just three silvers, you can take a swing at him! The only time you'll ever have a fair chance at taking on a ryrik."

Jace tugged against his chains and ground through his teeth, "I'm not a ryrik; only half."

Jasper turned on him. "Well, today I say you are."

As much as Jace wanted to argue, it mattered little what blood he did or did not have. The only thing that did matter was one fact—he was a slave. Jasper could do or call him whatever he pleased. Never had Jace so hated being another man's property. The hard look Jasper speared him with just before turning back to the crowd warned Jace of severe consequences if he failed to keep his mouth shut. Jace locked his jaw, but a hatred rose up inside him—the same sort of hatred he'd had for Dane. He tried to stop it, but it remained rooted inside him.

"You, sir," Jasper called out to a man nearby. "Why not prove your mettle to your lady? Do you know what a beast like this would do to her, given the chance?"

The woman holding the man's arm gasped and shrank closer to him, her hand to her throat. The fear and disgust with which she looked at Jace cut like a knife. Having lived all his life in conditions where men and women were housed together and no one cared what happened to slaves, he had seen things he wished he could blot out. How dare Jasper suggest he would do such a thing or speak of such vileness in a lady's presence. He would *never* harm or take advantage of a woman. Not for anything.

However, this woman would never know that; not even if he tried to tell her. No one would ever trust him.

Though Jace wasn't sure how hitting someone who couldn't fight back proved anything, the man apparently liked the idea. He promptly dug into his money pouch and fished out a couple of silver coins for Jasper. With a few of the other nearby townspeople cheering him on, the man approached Jace, a bit leery at first, but he quickly gained confidence. He drew back his fist. Jace tensed for the blow.

His head snapped to the side as the man's fist connected with his jaw. It wasn't as hard as one of Dane's punches, but it still rang in Jace's ears. All around, men whooped and cheered. Jace hung his head. So this was his life now—a spectacle and object of abuse to earn his master money.

JACE DREW A bucket of water from the well and glanced at his reflection as he set it on the edge. The bruises on his face had nearly faded, except for a slight shadow under his right eye. He sighed. That meant Jasper would soon take him out again. It had become the routine for the past two months. Take the half-blood out to one town or another, let the men pay to hit him until he was too bruised and battered to continue, let him recover, and then start all over again.

He splashed some of the water on his face, and then turned for the stable to begin his morning chores—the only part of his life he could look forward to. Rohir had a welcoming nicker for him when he entered. Jace went to the horse's stall and offered him the treat he had saved. As the horse munched the small piece of hard roll, Jace rested his forehead against Rohir's.

Why couldn't Jasper just let him be the stable boy? He craved the solitude of time spent with the horses—time that did not involve the other slaves sneering or insulting him, or the condemning, disgusted gazes of citizens burning into him as they went about their free lives. People were cruel and careless. He would never trust them. He would rather be left alone to tend to the animals. At least they were dependable and had no knowledge of what he was. Jasper would never allow him such peace. The man was about as cruel as they came.

"Half-blood."

Jace jerked and looked up at the sound of Zar's voice, his stomach clenching.

Zar gestured to one of Jasper's draft horses. "Get them fed and hitched to the wagon."

Jace gave a brief nod and let a slow breath seep out as Zar left the stable. So they would be heading out somewhere new—no doubt to some gladiator event, where Jasper's men would face off against other fighters in an arena. And Jasper would take Jace to earn some extra coin in the market squares. He always did.

Jace fed the two large draft horses first this morning, and then went on to feed and clean up after the others. When the animals had finished their hay and grain, he led them out to the courtyard where the wagon was waiting. The top half was barred, while the bottom planks were painted red and sported a white message he didn't know how to read. Jace hated the sight of it as much as he hated riding in it like a caged animal.

As he backed the horses up to the wagon to attach their harnesses, Jasper's house slaves bustled around with supplies. A lot of supplies. Apparently, this wasn't just a quick trip to a neighboring town. Nearby, a group of Jasper's best gladiators mingled. They seemed excited and ready for action. How could anyone be excited to enter an arena and fight another person, quite possibly to the death? The idea turned Jace's stomach and brought Dane's face to mind like a haunting presence.

Every time he remembered what he did, he wanted to be sick. It was a permanent weight he carried now.

Shortly after Jace finished hitching the team, Jasper marched out of his house with Zar and barked orders to the house slaves, who scurried to load the wagon. Next, he ordered the gladiators into the wagon. Jace stayed near the horses as each of the men climbed up and claimed their seats on the benches along either side of the wagon. After the last man entered, Jasper turned, and his mud-brown eyes locked on Jace.

"You too. Inside."

Jace let his shoulders sag. He hadn't truly believed Jasper would leave him behind, but some seed of desperation had hoped. He climbed in, and Jasper slammed the barred door shut behind him. Glancing at the other gladiators, Jace took a seat against the door. Though there was room on the benches, the looks the men cast him were clear—he wasn't welcome to join them. Instead, he was relegated to the floor like a dog.

With a long sigh, he rested his head against the bars and settled in to see where Jasper would take them this time.

Jace stared out of the wagon, taking in the sight with wide eyes. Valcré, the capital city of Arcacia. He had never seen anything like it—so many buildings and people. A couple of the eight men in the wagon with him looked in awe as well, while the others appeared to have seen it before.

Jace's heart beat a hard rhythm, and his palms sweated as he gripped the bars through which he watched the many people passing by on either side of the wagon. People from all stations of life. If there were so many on just one street, how many might be present in a market? The urge to shrink back out of sight gripped Jace. Jasper had brought him for one reason only—to put him on display. His jaw ached in anticipation of the abuse to come, but the thought of so many staring eyes hurt the most. There would be thousands of them, and he would be powerless to shield himself from their hatred.

He sank to the floor. If he could wish away the city and Jasper and every other person in Ilyon, he would. Or perhaps it would be better to wish away his own existence.

The wagon rolled slowly through the city for a good twenty minutes or more, until Jasper finally drew it to a halt. The men shifted on their benches to peer out. One of Jasper's foremost gladiators grinned through his thick black beard. "This is it, boys. This is where we'll either die or make names for ourselves. This ain't no small country arena. Here we'll be fighting in front of the emperor himself."

Jace leaned toward the side and caught a glimpse of the edge of a large arena. The ornate stone walls rose four stories high and appeared to occupy an area the size of a whole city block. The crowd here was particularly thick, buzzing with conversation. Scanning the people, Jace found many other barred wagons and gladiators, whose masters led them inside.

In a moment, Jasper appeared at the back of the wagon to let the gladiators out. When Jace moved to follow, Jasper shook his head. "You stay here."

He shut the door in Jace's face and turned his attention to the gladiators. Jace watched them all head toward the arena and gave a snort. He didn't want to join them anyway. Moving to the front of the wagon where he wouldn't be so noticeable, he took a seat on one of the benches and stretched his legs out along the length of it. He closed his eyes. He hadn't slept well on the four-day journey to Valcré, so it wasn't difficult to drift off.

Sometime later, Jace jerked awake to the sound of the wagon door opening. "Get up, half-blood. Time to earn your keep."

Jace bit back a grumble as he glowered at Jasper. The man was in too good a mood and had that money-hungry gleam in his eyes. His stomach cramped with both hunger and dread. He glanced out at the sun. It was around noon. The markets were sure to be busy this time of day.

Jace forced himself to his feet and stepped out of the wagon. Zar promptly attached his collar, and Jasper handed over his usual outfit, including a leather tie for his hair. Though every sense of self-preservation shouted in protest, he changed without arguing. The first and last time he had tried to resist, he'd not only had to face the crowds and their abuse, but had earned a beating from Jasper as well. While the man refrained from using the severe, flesh-tearing whips Jace so hated, in order to avoid long-lasting injuries to his slaves, it didn't lessen the biting sting of the horsewhip he always carried with him.

Jasper led the way, and Zar towed Jace along behind as they set out deeper into the city. With an unobstructed view, Jace gazed around at the architecture lining each street they traveled. Some of the buildings were constructed of wood and plastered walls, while others were of solid stone. The signs hanging over the streets boasted of just about every business imaginable.

In one of the narrower, shady streets rose a tall building where two women in tightly-cinched, low-cut dresses sashayed out into the street and beckoned to the male passersby. One, whose plump lips were painted a glaring shade of red, gave Jace a seductive smile and trailed her long fingers across his bare shoulder. He flinched and hurried ahead, his neck and cheeks growing hot. Zar released a low chuckle, and Jace sent him a glare. He breathed a little easier when they left the street and the women behind, but he had to wonder; did those women have any choice in what they were doing, or were they just as much slaves as he was? It appeared that the city was just like all the masters he had known—grand and self-important on the outside, while corrupt and cruel on the inside. They had little care for the lives that they ruined as they remained comfortable and in power.

They walked on for another fifteen minutes before the increased commotion of voices drew Jace from his moody thoughts. Ahead, he spotted colorful awnings and a bustling of people that signaled a market. Already the familiar shouts of merchants hawking their wares rose above the commotion.

When they entered the market, Jace found it situated in a huge city square that held four times the number of merchant stalls he had seen anywhere else. But the incredible array of goods didn't hold his attention. To the west, his gaze rose to a grand structure that overlooked the city—a huge, gold-hued palace.

"Yes, that's Auréa Palace," Jasper said, catching him staring. "The home of Emperor Daican."

Jace glanced at him, but gave the palace one more look. How could one man own all that, when others like Jace didn't have a single possession that actually belonged to them?

On the far side of the square, they found an open spot near a merchant selling a variety of hand pies. The savory scent flooded Jace's mouth with moisture. The only time he had ever come close to tasting such food was as a small child when the old cook had given him leftovers once in a while. Even that was nothing compared to the food offered in this market. His stomach growled.

"This should do nicely." Jasper nodded to Zar. "We'll get the crowd coming from the food carts."

Zar pounded the stakes into the ground between the cobblestones, and chained Jace to them. It took a little time for people to notice them, but soon Jasper's calls of "ryrik" drew a crowd. Then it began. Men handed over their coins to Jasper's greedy fingers and lined up for their turn to hit Jace. Some punches didn't have much power behind them, thrown by portly merchants and lesser nobles who had probably never been in a fight in their lives. Others, however, left pain shooting through his skull or lancing across his ribs. It wasn't long before the area around his eyes and lips started to swell. A couple of times, he almost fell to his knees, but he managed to stay upright and continued taking the hits.

About an hour after their arrival, Jace picked out a man heading their way. His brawny arms, wide chest, and tradesman clothing made him stand out from most of the people. He looked like a man who could deal serious damage, and Jace's heart pumped hard in warning. When the man reached Jasper, he handed over not a couple of silver coins, but a gold coin. Jace's stomach wrenched, as if taking a blow already. The man had paid for multiple swings, and Jasper was more than happy to let him, judging by the grin he flashed as he pocketed the valuable coin.

Jace's muscles went taut as the big man approached him, pushing up his sleeves. Everything inside him screamed to duck as the man prepared to swing, but he had already learned that such a move only earned him extra blows. Better to stand and take it and get it over with.

The first blow crashed into his face and sent him staggering. His chains jerked tight, and he fell to one knee. His ears buzzed, and his vision swam. He shook his head. Three bright red spots appeared on the stone below him as wetness dripped down his chin. Warmth seeped like hot oil through his veins. He tried to ignore it and pushed back to his feet where the man waited to take full advantage of what he had paid for. All around, the growing crowd egged him on.

Jace met his eyes and the cruel enjoyment in them. What made people enjoy hurting others so much?

The second blow hammered his ribs and forced the breath from his lungs. He grabbed for his chest and didn't even realize he was on his knees until he reached out to brace himself against the stones to keep from going all the way down. He couldn't breathe. Flames burst to life inside his chest. They surged through his blood, igniting the defiance he always had to bury.

He rose slowly, feigning a cowering surrender.

The man stepped closer. "Not so tough, are you, *ryrik*?"

He had barely ground out the word when Jace acted. Raising his elbow, he smashed it into the man's head with all the power of the heat raging within him. The man stumbled back, and blood poured from his nose. Jace froze in place, Dane's face flashing before him. *Not again!* He took a step forward to see if the man was all right, but something hard smashed against his skull, and he went down in a heap, consciousness fading.

Jasper's sharp curses roused Jace. He squinted into the sun that was exactly where it had been when he'd fallen. A flurry of footsteps and panicked voices told him he had only been out for a moment. Something tugged on his wrist, and he looked over to find Zar unchaining him. He then grabbed his shoulder and yanked him forward. "Get up."

Jace stumbled, his head spinning. He might not have kept his feet if Zar had not held him in place. The side of his head burned and oozed. Zar must have hit him with the butt of his dagger. He blinked hard to right his vision. A few feet ahead, blood spattered the stones. He gulped and tried to speak, but his tongue didn't seem to remember how to work. He looked around, but it only made him dizzy again. With a grimace, he squeezed his eyes shut. They popped open again when Zar jerked on his collar. He staggered forward as Jasper led the way quickly through the square.

"That man," Jace managed at last, "is he . . . all right?" His gut twisted into a painful knot.

Jasper sent a semi-disgusted look back at him. Jace would have expected him to be livid. Still, he didn't have any hope of escaping a sound beating for what he had done.

"If you want to call a broken nose all right."

The air released in a gush from Jace's lungs. A broken nose. At least he wasn't dead.

They marched through the city without stopping. Most of it was a hazy blur to Jace that he struggled to recall. By the time they reached the wagon back at the arena, his senses finally seemed to right themselves, though his head throbbed. Jasper removed the collar from his neck and shoved him to the open wagon door. Jace climbed inside, welcoming the escape from the crowds. Instead of slamming the door shut, Jasper peered in at him, much the same as on the day when he had first bought Jace.

"So you feel like fighting back, do you? Well, once we get home, I can arrange that."

JACE COULDN'T SAY he was glad to make it back to Jasper's place but, as much as he hated his cell, it was better than being chained to the other gladiators when they camped at night. And at least he could visit Rohir.

When the wagon halted inside the courtyard and Zar had closed the gate, Jasper let everyone out. However, they were missing two men who had died in Valcré's arena. Jace exited the wagon last, wincing as he ducked through the door. The welts from the beating he had known Jasper would give him still stung under the rough cloth of his shirt, and bruises covered his ribs from the blows in the square.

"Get the horses unhitched and settled, and then get your supper, or you'll be headed to your cell without it," Jasper told him.

Jace went right to work. The courtyard had already fallen into twilight, which left him little time. He hurried to unhitch the team, and led the horses into the stable. Once he had brushed and fed them and put the harnesses in their proper place, he paused at Rohir's stall. Even if he did miss supper, a moment with the horse calmed him—calm he hadn't found since before that first day in Valcré. He had not forgotten what Jasper had told him right after the incident in the square. The unease gnawed at him, and wouldn't abate until he found out exactly what Jasper had in mind for him.

He just stood and stroked Rohir's neck for a minute or two before he reluctantly turned to leave. The usual rowdy voices came from the mess hall. No doubt tonight would be full of tales of their exploits in the arena. Jace had already heard enough of it on the trip back, but he entered the hall and received his portion of supper from the cook.

Taking his bowl of lukewarm stew, he walked out and sat on the step of the hall. He stirred his spoon through the gravy and took a bite. As he chewed the tough meat, he looked at the light glowing through the windows of Jasper's house. He was probably sitting at his table, being waited on and eating the sort of food Jace had seen in Valcré.

A burn swirled up around his heart. He shook his head and swallowed hard. That heat was dangerous. Growing up, he had heard of ryrik rage, but he had never expected to have it grip him. Yet it did, and it seemed to flare to life more and more easily.

He looked at the gate. If only he could escape this life, maybe it would get better . . . but such an attempt might mean hurting or even killing someone. Every time he had tried to defend or stand up for himself, it had led to that. Did he dare risk it? Could he even trust himself? He had already killed one man and injured another. His throat swelled and ached as his deep inner voice condemned him with the one word he had tried not to let define him—*monster*. How could it be that he had fallen so far as to deserve it?

A throaty chirp startled him from his thoughts, and he

blinked the glaze from his eyes. He looked down along the side of the mess hall. A bird—some sort of jay with deep blue and charcoal feathers—stood there. He moved to get a closer look, and the bird hopped away from him unsteadily, its wing dragging along the ground.

Memories flitted into Jace's mind of the baby bird under the willow tree, something he hadn't thought about in a long time. The sight of this bird stirred the same desire to help that had gotten him into so much trouble that day as a little boy. He should just leave it alone. What did he know of repairing an injured wing, anyway? He turned his attention back to his stew and took a few more bites, but his gaze kept straying to the injured jay. Heaving a sigh, he finally pushed to his feet and walked into the mess hall.

After handing his empty bowl over to the cook, he walked out again. The jay had hopped a few more feet from the mess hall. Jace strode toward it. The bird flapped its good wing in an attempt to escape, but ended up falling on its side. Jace bent down and carefully scooped it into his hands. Glancing over his shoulder, he hurried to the stable. Zar would be out any minute to get everyone into their cells for the night.

Inside the stable, Jace grabbed a nearly empty grain sack and climbed up into the loft, where he set the jay gently in a pile of straw. He then ripped a strip of cloth from the sack before reaching for the jay again. Slowly, he maneuvered its injured wing into place. The bird squawked and struggled, but Jace managed to get the cloth strip wrapped around its body, securing the injured wing. Whether or not it would stay in place and heal properly, he couldn't say, but it was the best he could do.

Creating a small, nest-like area in the straw, he settled

the jay down and scooped a handful of grain from the sack to set next to it. Commotion came from outside, and Zar called for him.

Able to do nothing more for the bird, he scrambled down from the loft and hurried out to join the line of men heading down to their cells. Zar gave him a suspicious look as he passed, but Jace ducked his head and went on. In his cell, he sank down on his straw pallet and reached for the wool blankets Zar had given him. With fall drawing in, the nights had grown cold. Pulling them up over his shoulder, he closed his eyes. The weariness of the last few days settled on him heavily, yet sleep didn't come immediately as thoughts of the bird and hopes that it would survive crowded his mind.

Jace groaned at the sound of the rooster the next morning, his bruised ribs smarting. He rolled to his back, but that wasn't much better. Pushing up slowly, he rubbed the remnants of sleep from his eyes. His ribs still throbbed, but eventually the pain dulled.

In another moment, Zar appeared to let them all out. Impatience to leave his cell and get to the stable grew inside Jace. He fully expected the jay to have died during the night, but he still hoped. He let the other gladiators go ahead of him, as usual, but, once they reached the courtyard, he headed straight to the stable. Passing Rohir's stall, he braced himself and climbed up to the loft. At the top of the ladder, he lifted his brows. The jay stood there alertly, and much of the grain he had left was gone. This bird was more of a fighter than he'd thought.

He climbed down again and dug around in one of the supply corners until he found two old, chipped wooden bowls. One he filled with more grain and the other with water and set them up in the loft for the jay. He then hurried on with the rest of his chores before Zar could catch him wasting time. As he moved from stall to stall, tiny claws scratched against wood as the jay hopped around above him. Once, when he looked up, the bird was perched on the edge of the loft, peering down at him. It would need a name if Jace was going to keep taking care of him. He contemplated it while he finished cleaning the stalls. Finally, he looked up at the bird again.

"Strune."

The jay tipped its head, as if responding, and Jace nodded. The name had belonged to one of his previous master's young stallions and seemed a good fit.

When Jace finished his chores, he climbed back up into the loft to make sure Strune's bandage was secure. The jay was still leery of him, but didn't struggle quite as much when he picked him up. He was on his way down the ladder again when Zar's voice called from outside.

Jace drew a deep breath, gut-instinct warning him that today wouldn't be pleasant. He stepped outside and found both Zar and Jasper standing at the edge of the sandy area where the gladiators practiced.

"Yes?" He eyed Jasper warily, casting a quick glance at the wooden practice sword in Zar's hand.

Jasper turned to him, his fists on his hips, and tipped his head up as if he could peer down at Jace. He then gestured to a rack of practice weapons nearby. "Choose one."

Jace scrunched his brows together. "What?"

"Choose a weapon."

Jace looked at them, the coiling sensation in his middle tightening. "Why?"

"You proved in Valcré that it's time to train you for what I bought you for in the first place. Congratulations; you've graduated to gladiator-in-training."

Jace went stiff. A gladiator? He'd do almost anything, but fighting men, sometimes to the death, he would not. He had killed a man once—he would not do it again. Just the memories made him ill. He didn't even want the skill to be able to fight or kill other opponents. He was dangerous enough already.

Looking Jasper in the eye, he stood his ground. It would surely earn him a beating, but he would not let this man turn him into a trained killer. "No."

Jasper's lips curled in a malicious half-smile. "I figured you'd resist."

Wood cracked hard across Jace's back. He stumbled forward and groaned, glancing back at Zar. The man's stony expression offered no remorse. Then his attention jumped back to Jasper, who said, "You will either take up a weapon to defend yourself, or you can take the beating. Your stubbornness might last through today, but you will be out here every day to either fight or take your beating. It's your choice."

He didn't even give Jace a chance to think about it. Zar strode at him with the wooden sword. Jace raised his arms to protect his head, but it left his ribs exposed to the blow. He bit back a cry as the wood met bone. Doubling over, he struggled to get away, but the blows continued to pelt his body—his back, his arms, his chest. After the fifth blow, the fire ignited inside him, flushing his limbs with heat. He cursed it, fighting to make it stop, but, with every stringing crack of the wood against his flesh, it only burned hotter. How could he do this day after day?

He ground his teeth. He wouldn't give in. He wouldn't be the monster. The wooden sword smashed against his knee. It collapsed, and he fell into the sand. Even then, the blows continued. *Stop!* his body screamed. He had to endure this. He couldn't surrender to Jasper and let him turn him into the thing he so feared. His heart beat like it never had before, sending a surge of boiling heat through his veins as pain pulsated from every swelling bruise.

He couldn't take it anymore. Scrambling to his feet, he lunged for the weapons rack. He closed his fingers around the hilt of a wooden sword and spun around, slamming it into Zar's sword. A painful jolt passed through Jace's hands and up into his arm as the crack of the wood echoed in the courtyard. Zar stepped back. Jace gasped for breath as sweat poured down his battered body.

Jasper stepped into view. "The long sword, huh? Excellent."

His arms shaking, Jace looked down at the weapon, and then back to his master.

"Of all the weapons you could have chosen, that's the one you grabbed to defend yourself." Jasper nodded. "It suits you."

Jace dropped the sword, as if the hilt was searing into his hands. He shook his head, fighting with everything inside him to make the burn leave his chest. "No. I won't do it." His lungs heaved in desperation. "I won't fight for you."

Jasper stepped closer. "Oh, you will. You just proved it. So, for the next few months, you will be out here training every day with the men. If you want a repeat of this morning, that is your choice, but you *will* learn. Come this spring, you will put what you learn to use in the arenas."

JACE SWUNG HIS sword upward, and it met Zar's with a resounding crack. Immediately, he sidestepped, the cool sand shifting beneath his feet. Keep moving. That's what Jasper and Zar always drilled into him. Keep moving. He swiped at Zar's knees, but, despite his size, the man was quick, blocking the attack. Jace had been close, though. One of these times, he would hit his target. They traded several blows in rapid succession.

Heat twisted through Jace's body. Not as searing as when he was angry or in pain, but just enough to sharpen his senses and give him strength and energy he didn't have otherwise. He loathed it, but it was impossible to stop. It was as much a part of how his body functioned as breathing.

A bead of sweat rolled down near his eye, but he never took his attention away from Zar. The man breathed just as heavily, and his shirt had grown dark with moisture. It had taken months, but Jace could finally hold his own against his highly-skilled trainer.

He had barely allowed himself such a thought before Zar launched a brutal attack. Though caught off guard, he managed to block each strike until Zar's sword smashed into his shoulder. He groaned through his teeth. Several choice words he heard regularly sprang to mind, but he shook them away. Jasper might force him to fight, but he couldn't force him to become a crass brute like the others. It was one of the only things he had any say in.

The fire in his blood that had flared with the hit quickly dulled the pain. Jace set his jaw and raised his sword to face Zar again, but then caught sight of Jasper.

"That's enough," his master called. When he neared, he looked Jace up and down. "Very good." He had lingered around the practice area a lot lately, watching everyone, particularly Jace. "Yes, I think you're ready. Zar, call the rest of the men."

Jace breathed hard to catch his breath as the rest of the men gathered, willing the heat inside him to cool. However, a prickling sensation took its place. None of Jasper's announcements ever boded well. When all was quiet, their master spoke.

"Men, you've spent the last several months training hard. Now it's time to prove your skills. Tomorrow we will be heading out to our first games of the year."

Anticipation rippled through the group. Several of the men even grinned and voiced their eagerness, but Jace's stomach soured. The day he had dreaded for months had come.

"Take the remainder of the day to rest up and prepare yourselves," Jasper told them, which earned an even more enthusiastic response.

Though the men lingered and talked, Jace trudged alone toward the well. Along the way, he breathed in deeply. The air had a certain freshness to it in the spring, when it was still cool enough to cut the stench of the city that would rise with the temperature. That was one thing he missed about the previous estates he had belonged to—being out in nature. He hated the months spent caged up inside Jasper's courtyard. He had to admit, though, that Jasper had better housing for his slaves. The cells were cold, but fully sheltered from the raw winds the winter had brought, and Jasper provided them with plenty of warm clothes and blankets. Not that he cared about anything more than protecting his investments.

Jace drew water from the well and drank deeply. The winter nights might not have been so bad, but he had hated the days. True to his word, Jasper had him practice with Zar every day. Some days he had chosen to resist, desperate not to become a fighter, but the beatings were too much. Every time, they broke his will, and he found himself giving in. Now, after those miserable months, he knew more about wielding a sword than he had ever imagined.

Flapping wings rustled overhead. Strune fluttered down in front of him and landed on the rim of the bucket. He looked into the water and then up at Jace, tipping his head first one way and then the other in his quick bird movements. He hopped around the rim toward Jace's hand, as if expecting him to produce a handful of grain right there.

"I don't have anything with me." Jace ran his finger along the silky gray and blue feathers of Strune's back. The jay gave a cackling chirp and flitted upward, landing on Jace's shoulder—his usual place when Jace wasn't busy practicing. Jace hadn't truly expected the jay to survive or ever fly again, but, over the winter, his wing had healed. Though his flight was a little awkward now, he could get around just fine. Even so, he hung around Jace, probably for the easy food, though Jace liked to think it was more than that.

The jay had become a familiar part of life here in Jasper's slave quarters. Even the other gladiators were amused by the bird. They still regarded Jace as nothing more than a half-blood animal, but having Strune bridged some of the widest gaps between them. Most of the hostility toward him had subsided to cool indifference.

While the rest of the men would lounge around, trading stories and an odd combination of insults and compliments for the rest of the day, Jace would not join them. Deep inside, he longed for such camaraderie, but they would never accept him that way, so he didn't even try. Instead, he headed toward the stable with Strune, where their only other companions resided.

Rohir nickered when he walked in. Jace dug a handful of grain out of the sack by the door and gave most of it to the horse, letting Strune hop down his arm to take the rest. Once the jay resumed his spot on his shoulder, Jace got a brush and entered Rohir's stall. The motion of sliding the brush over Rohir's coat soothed Jace. He tried to lose himself in it and not think of what was to come when he faced his first opponent in the arena, but he had heard so many gory stories from the others that he had a hard time stopping his imagination from creating the scene.

The haunting image of Dane's lifeless face floated in. He ground his teeth together. If only he had never killed him. He would probably still be there, working in the fields. That one disturbing moment had made him dangerous, and Jasper had taken advantage of it, turning him into a weapon he could wield for profit. Jace shuddered. What type of world did they live in where men could get rich on the blood and pain of others? Were there any good people? He shook his head. The longer he lived, the less he believed it was possible.

A sharp pain pinched Jace's ear, and he jerked. "Ow!"

Strune launched off his shoulder, fluttering to the far side of the stall.

Jace glared at him and rubbed his ear. "What was that for?"

Strune tipped his tufted head and then preened his feathers, as if completely ignoring Jace. The smallest laugh rose within Jace, and he shook his head. The bird was a troublemaker, but he brought a little light to Jace's life that he hadn't known in a very long time.

Jace's stomach churned. In the stands overhead, the hum of voices suggested a large crowd. He swallowed hard to keep his stomach down, but his mouth wouldn't produce any moisture. Soon, all those people would have their eyes on him as he fought against another man—not with the wooden practice swords he had trained with, but a metal sword. A sword with a blade. A sword that could kill.

Jasper strode down the line of his gladiators with Zar in the dim, stifling waiting area of the arena, handing out equipment. When they reached Jace, Jasper gave him a dark brown, boiled-leather cuirass and pair of thick bracers. Jace did not ask questions or refuse. Not this time. He buckled on the cuirass over his sleeveless tunic, and Zar helped him with the bracers. When they finished, Jasper offered the hilt of a longsword. Now Jace did hesitate. He stared at the weapon.

Its construction was simple and unadorned, but that thin razor edge would be deadly.

Jasper speared him with a warning look. Jace finally reached up to wrap his fingers around the leather hilt, and Jasper released the blade. The weight of the weapon sent an invisible blow to Jace's insides. Jasper stepped closer, his voice cool and harsh.

"I've made a big deal about your fight. Everyone wants to see the half-blood ryrik and what he can do, so, when you go out there, you better give them what they came to see. Do you understand?"

Jace met his eyes, holding them as all the hatred he had carried for this man for almost a year rose to the surface. Heat flushed his fingers gripping the sword. For a brief moment, he saw himself using the blade on Jasper and putting a stop to this, but he forced the thought away. He couldn't kill again. Not like that.

That vicious smile lifted the corners of Jasper's lips. "I know what you're thinking, half-blood. I can see it in your eyes and how that light burns in them. Just see to it that you take that fight you have inside out into the arena."

Crushing the sword hilt in his hand, Jace stood stone-still as Jasper strode away. He had never hated anyone like he hated Jasper. Not even Dane. It terrified him that, someday, he would go through with killing him. He wasn't sure if he would be able to stop himself; not when his blood was so quick to heat and drive him to act. His gaze slid to Zar. Though Jasper had walked off, the man still watched him with a knowing look. Jace would have to be faster than him if he were ever to attack their master.

The next hour or two of waiting stretched out in a miserable eternity. Each of Jasper's gladiators went out and then returned, all with either no or minor injuries, except for one young man. He was one of the newer gladiators, having arrived shortly after Jace. This had been his first fight too. When a few slaves carried his limp form inside, blood covered his chest and dripped into the sand at their feet. That one brief look told Jace he wasn't likely to survive. His middle squeezed so tightly he struggled to keep his stomach from coming up. He closed his eyes and gritted his teeth. He would not be afraid. Fear was weakness.

But it wormed through him anyway, like icy fingertips across his skin.

His heart rate rose, and tremors passed up and down his arms as he kept readjusting his grip on the longsword. It weighed about the same as the wooden practice sword, but, with every minute that passed, it seemed to gain a pound. This fight would be nothing like practice, where he would only receive a collection of painful bruises for failing to block an attack. His life depended on his ability to execute the moves he had learned.

The crowd's cheers erupted above him, signaling the end of another match.

"You're up, half-blood."

Jace almost choked on his heart at Zar's declaration. An instant freezing of his blood locked him in place. Zar gripped his arm and shoved him hard toward an upward-sloping tunnel. Jace fought to moderate his breathing, but it came in hard gasps. Bright sunlight shone at the end of the tunnel. He slowed, and Zar pushed him the rest of the way, nearly shoving him to his knees at the end. Jace stumbled forward, out into the arena.

His gaze darted from one side to the other. The circular area wasn't very large—about thirty feet in diameter—but the raised stands around it held a couple hundred people at least. And they all stared down at him. Murmurs of "half-blood" whispered in his ears. He made another failed attempt to swallow, and barely resisted the urge to turn back to the tunnel.

Then his gaze fell on a man standing directly across from him. He was almost twice Jace's age, though not any larger. He, too, carried a longsword. For a tense moment, neither of them moved. But then the man started forward, his steps certain and swift. Jace raised his sword; however, everything Zar had taught him suddenly vanished. He remembered nothing. The man bore down on him. His blade lifted and flashed in the sunlight. With a jarring crash, Jace met it with his.

He stumbled, scrambling to recover his skills. The man pursued and attacked again. Jace managed a block, but it threw him off balance. Over and over again, the man came at him. The only pulsing thought in Jace's mind was to defend himself. He didn't even try to find an opening to attack. The collision of metal against metal rang in his ears and numbed his hands. How could he keep this up? The fight wouldn't end until one of them came out victorious. His heart crashed against his ribs. He would not survive this. Jasper was wrong. He wasn't ready. He would *never* be ready.

Searing pain tore across his shoulder. He staggered away and gripped it. Warm wetness met his fingers, and he looked down. Blood trailed along his bare arm in thin streams of crimson. The sight of it and the pain were like oil to a flame. Heat burst through his chest and raced through his body. The pain faded, the panic disappeared, and his mind stilled. The barest crunch of sand reached his ears and set off a warning. He spun around, his sword upraised. It crashed against his opponent's. This time, the other gladiator stumbled under the force of Jace's attack. The stands of people faded away as Jace's focus narrowed in on his opponent. The fear that had crippled him now fueled the heat that propelled him forward.

Everything he had learned rushed back to him. Instinct and reflex took over. He attacked the man with a ferocity driven by the pulsing surge of his fire-infused blood. Though his opponent managed a few attacks of his own, Jace dominated, forcing the man to give ground. He had no idea how long the fight lasted; he just kept pressing forward. At one point, the man's blade sliced his leg, but a fresh burst of heat instantly swallowed the pain.

With the surge of strength it brought, he swiped the opposing sword to the side. The man backpedaled and tried for a second attack, but Jace sidestepped and lunged. His sword met a brief resistance, and then sank through the man's chest armor. The man gasped. Their gazes met, and the roaring of blood in Jace's head grew silent as he watched the light fade from his opponent's eyes. The man's legs buckled, and he collapsed at Jace's feet, pulling the sword from Jace's hands.

Jace could only stare as the man's lifeblood pooled on his breastplate around the sword, reflecting the white clouds overhead. The breath gusted from Jace's lungs as his own legs gave out. His knees hit the sand, but still his eyes remained fixed on the man, unblinking. *I killed him. I'm a killer.* He had done it again. He was a monster.

As if just coming to, a loud sound rushed in around him like a blast of stormy wind—cheers. He looked up. The spectators were *cheering*. He'd killed a man, and they lauded him for it. He wanted to scream at them. How could they enjoy this?

Nothing in his body seemed to work. His gaze dropped back to his slain opponent. The fact of what he had done seemed to tear a chunk out of his heart, leaving it raw and bleeding. If this was the life Jasper forced on him, would he have any heart left when he finally met his own end? Would he have anything left but that awful raging blood and the mental scars of the people he would kill?

Rough hands gripped him and dragged him up. He vaguely heard Zar grumbling as he stumbled toward the tunnel. Back inside, Jasper waited for him, with a sickening smile of pleasure.

"Well done. You did exactly as I'd hoped. Keep it up, and you'll soon make a name for yourself."

The paralysis that had gripped Jace in the arena broke free. He lunged toward Jasper, but Zar seized his shoulder and held him back.

"You're an animal!" Jace shouted. "How could you make me do that?"

"*I'm* an animal?" Jasper laughed, but his voice was low and harsh. "No, Jace, you're the animal—the monster—and that's what will make me rich."

He chuckled again and turned away. Jace clenched his fists, but Zar's hand tightened. His chest shuddering, Jace yelled after Jasper, "I won't fight again!"

Jasper paused, and then spun on his heel. He marched back to Jace, his eyes cruel and cold. "Then you will die. If you're not killed outright during a fight, I will make sure every officiator of every game we attend knows to call for your death if you're defeated and survive to the end of the match. And, in case that starts to sound preferable to fighting, just consider this—what do you think happens to those who die without souls?"

JACE SAT ON a bench in his cell underneath the arena stands and stared at the floor. The roar of the cheers, the pounding of feet, his own heartbeat—they meshed together in a pulsing buzz around him and created a backdrop for Jasper's words echoing in his head from that morning. *"One year, half-blood. That's how long you've been a gladiator."*

One year.

One year of fights, of blood, of death. It felt like a lifetime. It had taken him everywhere—from tiny rope-rimmed rings, where spectators stood around the perimeter, to large arenas, such as this one, that easily held thousands of people. He had even been to Valcré. Fought and won. He had not lost a single fight. Every victory had earned him just that much more fame. The people saw him as a frightening, yet fascinating, spectacle, just as Jasper knew they would. Invitations for Jace to fight poured in from everywhere, and Jasper rarely turned them down. Even when the other gladiators were allowed time to rest between fights, he continued to push Jace. If Jace wasn't bleeding or seriously wounded, then he could fight as far as Jasper was concerned.

Thirty-three opponents. Nineteen men dead. He would never forget a single one of them. Like Dane, they would haunt him and steal any hope of ever finding peace. He had become the fighter Jasper wanted. Everywhere they went, people knew of him—the half-blood ryrik. The more his skills increased, the more skilled his opponents became, but he no longer felt fear when he entered the arena. He no longer felt anything.

He lifted his eyes to the sound of footsteps carrying over the commotion above. Zar appeared and unlocked his cell. "You're up, half-blood."

Letting out a long breath, Jace stood. He took his familiar longsword from Zar's hand and strode through the tunnel and up into the arena. The crowd erupted, but he had learned to shut them out. In the middle of the sandy, bloodstained battlefield, he stopped and waited for his opponent. The man exited the opposite tunnel a moment later. Jace watched him, studying how he carried himself. He was a large man, with bulging arms. In one hand, he carried a massive sword that had to weigh twice what Jace's did. That would make him slow and possibly clumsy. His heavy metal armor would also slow him down. Jace's leather armor would do little to stop a blade such as the man carried, but it allowed him greater mobility and speed.

However, the way the man strode toward him, undaunted, told Jace he didn't expect to lose this fight. No, his eyes held the determination of a man who desired the distinction of being the first to defeat Jace.

Like curling heat from a flame, warmth worked through Jace's muscles. He didn't even try to stop it anymore. With a growl, the man rushed him, going for a quick kill. Jace jumped to the side. As the man's momentum took him past, Jace swung his sword and sliced open the back of his opponent's calf. The man stumbled, cursing. Vaguely, Jace heard the crowd's gasping reaction. Though the man didn't go down, his injury would help Jace disarm him and end the fight with as little bloodshed as possible. He would only kill if his own life depended on it.

Recklessly, the man charged him again. Jace blocked and dodged his attacks until the man's gasping breaths surrounded them and sweat rolled down his face. Whoever thought the man would be any match for Jace should lose his job, but at least Jace wouldn't have to kill him. When his opponent could barely find the strength raise his sword, Jace maneuvered himself into the right position and smashed the weapon out of his hand. Before the man could react, Jace kicked his legs out from under him. He landed with a crash on his back, and Jace placed the tip of his sword at the man's neck in victory.

He then raised his gaze to the stands and waited for the crowd and the officiator of the games to give him the sign of life so he could return to his cell.

But something happened. Something he had never seen before. All around the stands, the people jabbed their thumbs toward their throats. A chant rose up until soon the whole crowd joined in.

"*Kill, kill, kill!*"

The fire died in Jace's chest, and his blood turned cold. No crowd had ever called for death in one of his fights. They had always let his fallen opponents live. His gaze jumped to the officiator standing at the edge of his view box.

"Life, *please*," Jace gasped to himself.

The man jerked his thumb toward his throat. Jace's heart dropped into his stomach. *No.* He looked down at his fallen opponent. The man stared up at him, stone-faced, but his wide eyes betrayed his fear. The chant rose in volume around them. They would not let him leave this arena without bowing to their wishes. Even if he refused, he would then have to face Jasper. He swallowed hard. He had managed to avoid a beating for several months now.

The chanting from the stands blasted him from all sides, pounding inside his head while the thought of a beating tied his stomach in a knot. He raised his sword, poised for a strike. The crowd hushed in anticipation, and Jace's opponent closed his eyes. Jace squeezed the hilt of his sword, willing himself to bring it down. Yet, all at once, the face of every man he had killed bombarded him—their last breaths, their last moment of life before they fell before him.

He choked out a breath and stepped back. He would not do it. He would not kill an already- defeated and defenseless opponent. It didn't matter what Jasper would do to him. He had already made him into a killer, but Jace would not do it in cold blood.

Turning his back on his opponent, he crossed the arena to the tunnel. Halfway there, angry shouts and boos took the place of the chants that previously echoed from the stands. He looked to the entrance of the tunnel. Zar waited for him there. The grim look on his face told Jace that they both knew how livid Jasper would be. Jace drew a hard breath and tried to prepare himself.

Zar didn't say a word when Jace reached him, only led him back to his cell in heavy silence. Jace had barely entered the cell when the slap of approaching footsteps echoed in the hall. He turned. Jasper stormed toward the cell, his whip already in hand. Jace straightened to face him, steeling himself.

"What was that?" Jasper barged into the cell. "Why didn't you kill him?"

"He was already defeated."

"I don't care if he was on his knees, begging; I've told you to obey the crowd."

Jace squeezed his fists. "They've never called for death before. I couldn't just kill him in cold blood. And I won't just kill at your command."

Jasper's eyes narrowed. "If you don't give the crowds what they want, then we will cease to be invited to these games and I will *not* allow that. Your life belongs to me. You don't have a will of your own—you don't get to make choices. You will do *exactly* as I command." Jasper snapped his fingers at Zar. "Take his armor."

As Zar entered the cell, Jace held Jasper's gaze, the fight and defiance in his blood creeping in, but his heart pounded heavily in anticipation for what was to come.

The back end of the wagon rolled over a rut, tipping Jace off balance. His shoulder bumped the side and ignited the tender welts crisscrossing his back. He winced. Three times now in the last month he had defied Jasper and the crowds and let a defeated opponent live. And three times he had paid for it, enduring Jasper's wrath.

In another few minutes, the wagon hit cobblestone. He raised his eyes as they entered Jasper's courtyard. By now, the sun had sunk. He and the couple of other gladiators Jasper had taken out left the wagon as soon as Zar unlocked it. Light and voices drifted from the mess hall. The other gladiators headed over to get their supper, but Jace did not follow. Pain from his latest beating stole his appetite. Instead, he headed to the well to get a drink for his dry throat.

As he neared, Strune flew down from a tree just on the other side of the courtyard wall. He landed first on the well's crossbeam and then flew to Jace's shoulder.

"Hey," Jace murmured.

He stroked the bird's back. Like brushing Rohir, it helped relieve the ever-growing ache inside. At least animals like Strune and Rohir didn't know what he was or what kind of life he lived. They didn't understand death or killing. As hard as he tried to force them away, his thoughts turned to the fights. Could he continue to defy his master, or would he eventually, one day, give in? Already he felt worn thin. He grimaced. The thought of killing that way threatened to upend his stomach.

A door slammed and two sets of heavy footsteps approached. Jace spun around, apprehension prickling along the painful nerves in his back. Jasper and Zar both strode toward him. The dark look on Jasper's face proved he was still simmering over the outcome of the last fight. Jace tensed, the heat that always came in preparation for a fight stirring within him. Perhaps one beating had not been enough to appease Jasper, though Jace didn't see his whip.

Jasper stopped a few feet away, but Zar moved to Jace's side. Jace glanced at him. There was a pitying, almost regretful, look in his otherwise-hard expression. Suspicion running cold along Jace's skin, he turned his gaze to his master. The moment his attention left Zar, the man grabbed Strune from his shoulder. Jace reached out as the jay squawked, but Zar shoved him back against the well and handed Strune over to Jasper. Panic burst through Jace. He lunged for them, not caring what Jasper would do to him. He just had to get Strune free. Zar's arm caught him around the throat and held him in a chokehold. Jace struggled, but couldn't wrench himself free.

Finally, he stilled, but his chest heaved, and he glared at Jasper. "Let him go."

Jasper raised his brows, a cruel gleam in his eyes. Strune struggled in his grasp, pecking at his hands, but Jasper didn't seem to notice. "This bird means a lot to you, doesn't it?"

A clawing desperation tore through Jace's insides. "Please. Just let him go."

Jasper just stared at him for a moment and, then, in one swift second, he snapped Strune's neck.

Agony ripped a hole right through Jace's already ragged heart and turned his blood to molten metal that roared in his ears. Raw energy surged through his body. He reached for Jasper, yanking against Zar with a hoarse yell, but the pressure against his throat cut it short. He fought furiously, with only one raging desire—to get his hands around Jasper's neck. Zar's arm locked more tightly around his throat until shadows closed in around his vision. He couldn't breathe. His legs went weak, and his knees buckled.

Then his airway opened. He gulped for breath, his strength gone. The fire had faded, but the pain only grew. He shook with the agony of loss. Slowly, he raised his head as Jasper stepped closer, his voice cold and heartless.

"From now on, half-blood, you *will* do exactly as I command. And, until all hints of defiance are gone, you are banned from the stable. You will spend every waking moment of every day training to become the greatest gladiator Arcacia has ever seen. When you're not training, you will be in your cell. You will not have anything that even resembles freedom until you learn to do as you're told."

He dropped Strune at Jace's knees, and then he and Zar strode away.

For several long minutes, in which every sluggish beat of Jace's heart sent pain through his chest, he couldn't move. He could only stare at Strune's lifeless body. Tears welled, burning his eyes, and he shuddered with each hard breath. Finally, he scooped Strune into his hands, just like the little baby bird Nicolas and Teague had killed all those years ago.

"Please . . . move," he gasped out.

But the bird was gone.

Jace sagged against the well, the cold stones pressing into his swollen back. Strune had been the only thing he could call his own. He had *nothing*. Even his life was in the hands of others. Strune had been his, but, just as everything else, someone had come along and stolen him from Jace too. Now he couldn't even visit Rohir. Anything that had brought even the smallest spark of light to his life was gone, plunging him fully into the darkness he had fought for so long.

His chest heaving, he let out a loud cry. How far could he sink? How long until Jasper succeeded in breaking him completely?

"ALL RIGHT, OUT of the wagon."

Jace rose stiffly at Jasper's command. His entire body ached. Jasper had never worked him so hard in training. When Jasper did allow him to rest at night, he couldn't sleep without dreams and nightmares tormenting him. Each day it grew harder to want to defy Jasper. Surrender dragged at him. He just wasn't sure he cared anymore. Not since Jasper had killed Strune a few weeks ago. It had crushed Jace's will that night. Maybe he had none left.

He stepped down from the wagon. Jasper had only brought him along this time. Invitations for Jace were growing scarce with his reputation of disappointing the crowds. Now Jasper took any they could get.

Jace glanced around the open meadow, where Jasper and Zar had set up camp. A large city sprawled directly ahead and a forest behind them. Many other gladiator wagons occupied the meadow. Which of the men in those cages would he have to fight? He hated himself for it, but he couldn't help hoping it would be a simple, straightforward fight to the death—that he wouldn't even have to think about whether or not to kill his opponent.

Jasper handed over his armor. When he was ready, Zar attached his collar, and the three of them approached the city. The streets teemed with people and activity. Apparently, the games were popular here. He soon spotted the arena ahead, which drew people like bees to the hive. He hated all of them.

The arena, though large, certainly could use some repair work. The old wood didn't look entirely stable, but it could collapse on everyone, including him, for all he cared. It would be a mercy.

Inside the dark, musty interior, Jasper and Zar led him into the waiting area. Several other gladiators and their owners stood around. All eyes seemed to rest on Jace, and hostility emanated from their gazes. They knew who he was. He stared them down.

Jace didn't have long to wait. As he approached the tunnel, Jasper held him back.

"You'd better not disappoint this time." He delivered the warning with a promise in his eyes of severe retribution if Jace disobeyed again.

Jace held back a response and walked out. The crowd welcomed him with an eruption of cheers, though not as loudly as in the past. His opponent had already entered and waited near the center. Jace sized up the tall, blond-haired man. His weapons consisted of a short sword and large round shield. He wasn't used to facing fighters who carried a shield, but it didn't matter. Nothing mattered. Whether he won or lost, he didn't care.

Saluting the crowd, the man approached. Jace let him come, not taking a defensive stance until the man raised his sword to attack. Their blades crashed together. Jace pushed against him to throw him off balance. The sooner he could disarm him, the sooner the fight would end. However, the man pushed back. This time, Jace found himself backpedaling. He immediately took up his fighting stance again. This man had more skill than most Jace faced—perhaps by design. Maybe this fight was meant to be his last.

The man's sword arced toward him. Jace batted it off to the side and moved in for his own attack, but the man's shield bashed his shoulder. He stumbled. Before he could defend himself, the man slashed his arm. The crowd burst into cheers as pain shot through Jace's nerves and into his heart, where the fire exploded to life. It raged through him. With a shout, he pressed forward in attack.

Everything he had learned from Zar was put to the test. For every attack he launched, the other gladiator answered back. They circled around and around the arena. *Keep moving.* Zar's voice echoed in his mind. Every time they clashed, a new wave of cheers burst from the stands. Jace had never faced an opponent so evenly matched with him.

Sweat rolled down his face, stinging his eyes. He blinked rapidly, unwilling to take his eyes off his opponent. To do so would mean certain defeat. His senses were on fire, but fatigue weighed on his muscles. Had he ever fought so long before? Gasping breaths rattled from his chest and ached in his lungs. He had to disarm the man.

He raised his sword and swung down hard. His blade crashed into the other gladiator's shield and slid off. Before

Jace could raise it again in defense, the man struck. Jace spun away, but the blade sliced open his left forearm.

He sucked in his breath. Though he didn't know if he could fight much longer, the waning fire inside him flared at the pain in his arm. A fresh burst of energy surged through him. Raising his sword once more, he drove into his opponent, slashing at his shield, his sword, his legs. The man staggered backward, barely able to block. Jace did not stop pressing forward until, at the opposite side of the arena, the man lost his balance and fell hard at Jace's feet. He scrambled to his knees, but Jace stood over him in a heartbeat, his sword hovering over the man's shuddering chest.

It was over. He had won. Again.

He shifted his gaze to the people in the stands as he struggled to catch his breath. The fight had been a good one. Surely they would allow the man to live. However, one at a time, the people jabbed their thumbs toward their throats until the motion overtook the entire arena. With it came the death chant. Jace looked to the officiator, but had no hope. The man motioned for death and the crowd cheered.

Jace dropped his gaze back to the man at his feet. He stared up at Jace, waiting bravely. He had to admire that. The man had been a good fighter. Jace raised his sword a little higher as Jasper's warning flooded his mind. Maybe he should just do it. Did it even matter anymore? Jasper always got what he wanted, one way or another. He had made him a fighter, a killer, despite how he had battled it. He'd broken him down until he had given in. He would just do the same now, keep breaking him, a little bit at a time, until he couldn't resist anymore. Why fight any longer when the outcome wouldn't change in the end?

He gripped his sword hard. It would only take one thrust.

No. He bit down hard as the conflict rose within him. He couldn't kill in cold blood. But Jasper. He would break him. Somehow, he would find a way. Yet, what more did Jace have to lose? This choice right here was all he had. If he let Jasper take that from him, then he would have nothing. He would fully become the monster Jasper seemed determined to turn him into. A coldblooded, heartless killer. And maybe someday he would be. Maybe someday Jasper would win, but, for as long as he could, Jace would fight him.

Strengthened by this determination, Jace spun his sword around and drove the hilt into the side of the gladiator's head—not hard enough to be lethal, but enough to knock him momentarily senseless. As the man toppled to the ground, silence engulfed the arena just before the booing and jeers erupted. Jace turned in a slow circle and glared up at them. Animals. Monsters. How could they think of him as such when they were so vicious, sitting there, calling for death?

Tossing his sword aside, he strode toward the tunnel. Garbage pelted him along the way, but he did not look back. The fatigue of the fight descended on him as he stepped into the shadows. With it came the dread of facing Jasper and the beating that would no doubt rival all but the one he still wished he hadn't survived from his previous master.

Jasper was there the moment he stepped into the waiting area. His fist smashed into Jace's chin and sent him to his knees. Blood ran hot and fast from Jace's lip. Heat flushed through him, but it was weak and faded quickly. He didn't even want to fight anymore. Let Jasper have his retribution.

Jace stumbled after Zar as Jasper stormed out of the arena. Exhaustion dragged at him, and his wounds throbbed, but the worst was how dead he felt inside. He hadn't even killed the man, but today seemed to mark yet another step deeper into the torturous black pit of his life. A life that would only grow blacker and more painful as Jasper continued to break down his will.

At the wagon, Zar chained Jace's wrist to a stake he had driven into the ground earlier. He then took his armor, leaving him exposed and defenseless. As soon as he finished, Jasper stepped up and plowed his fist into Jace's unprotected ribs. The air gusted from Jace's lungs, and he went to his knees again, where he was most vulnerable, but he was too spent to try to get up.

The whip struck hard, burning the skin beneath his thin tunic. He choked back a reaction to the pain before it struck again. And again. Screaming out curses, Jasper brought the whip down over and over.

"You pathetic, worthless creature! I'll teach you to defy me! When will you learn to do as you're told?"

Jace ground his teeth together. Why did he do this? Why did he keep winning? Keep walking out of the arena only to face this torture and misery? What made him persist?

Nothing.

The word settled with heavy finality in his mind. The whip forced a groan farther up his throat. Right there, right then, he decided. He wouldn't walk out next time. It was time to end this. He had suffered through this life for too long. It needed to end. Whatever happened beyond this life, he didn't care anymore. He only knew he could not do this any longer.

He hunched forward, waiting for Jasper to exhaust his wrath, biting down on the pain that was determined to loosen his tongue. He would not cry out—he would not show weakness in front of this man. Never again. He only needed to endure. Endure tonight and the days until his next fight, and then it would all be over. Maybe he could even get his hands on a blade before then and end it himself. He raised his head just enough to glance toward Zar and the large dagger on his belt. Jace might just be quick enough to grab it and use it before Zar could stop him.

Jasper's fingers grabbed at Jace's hair and jerked his head up. Jace glared into the man's livid face.

"How many times do I have to tell you? You could be a sensation. You please the crowd, do you understand?"

The back of his hand smacked across Jace's face, and something snapped inside Jace. He was going to kill this man. He shoved to his feet, but his fatigue slowed his usual speed, and Jasper was ready for him. Another blow to Jace's ribs had him back on his knees, gasping for breath. *Just finish with me!* He wanted to scream. He wanted to die.

"Excuse me." The voice came unfamiliar but commanding before another whip strike could fall. Jasper spun around, and Jace looked up. Nearby, a man dismounted a sturdy white gelding and marched toward them. He was older than Jasper by a good ten or fifteen years, judging by his graying hair and beard, yet he carried himself with impressive confidence, considering Zar stood at the wagon close by, his hand near his sword.

"What's the meaning of this?" the man demanded.

"None of your business. He's my slave."

The man glared down at Jasper. "Slave or not, no man should be treated in such a manner."

The declaration sent a shock straight into Jace's core, but Jasper let out a cruel bark of laughter. "He's no man."

He reached for Jace's hair and yanked it up to reveal one of Jace's ears. The shock faded as humiliation twisted Jace's insides.

Giving the man an adequate look, Jasper shoved Jace's head away. "He's half ryrik."

Jace looked up again, locking eyes with the man, who stared at him. *Yes, look at me. The monster.* Jasper was right. He wasn't a man. He was an animal.

"He gets just what he deserves. Now, go about your own business."

The man broke eye contact with Jace. He would walk away now, realizing his mistake. Jace didn't deserve his pity or intervention.

Jasper raised the whip again. Jace ducked his head, his muscles tightening. *Just get it over with.* Once Jasper finished with his tirade, Jace would end the pain forever.

"Enough!"

The stranger's voice drew Jace's gaze up once more. The man had caught the whip in his hand. Why? Why would he intervene? It would only make Jasper more furious. Scowling, Jasper tugged on the whip, but the man held fast. Jasper balled his fist and swung at the man's chin. Jace almost jumped up to stop him, but, before he could, the man caught Jasper by the wrist. With practiced ease, he twisted it around. Jasper landed on his back with a gasp, and Jace's eyes went wide. No one had ever done such a thing to Jasper before. Zar yanked out his sword and stepped forward, but the stranger reacted just as quickly. He pulled out his own sword and set it against Jasper's throat. Zar paused.

"This is between me and him," the man said with a glare.

To Jace's surprise, Zar remained where he was. How did one man command such obedience, even from a brute like Zar? Jace looked at the stranger again, who let Jasper scramble to his feet and fumble for the sword he always carried for show.

"How much do you want for him?"

The stranger's question left a deafening silence inside Jace. The man wanted to buy him? Why? What cruel purpose could he have in mind? Then again, what could possibly be worse than the life he was living already? He shook his head to himself. Every time he thought that, it *did* get worse. Would this just be the next step deeper into that pit? No, he would die first. One way or another, he would end it before he could suffer further.

Jasper's face scrunched in confusion. "What?"

"How much do you want for the boy?"

Jasper looked at Jace, eyeing him up and down, judging his worth, while his greedy mind went to work. Jace gave him a cold look, and then the other man.

Jasper let out another harsh laugh as he faced the stranger again. "You'd pay for such an animal?"

Jace winced. Why did it still sting so much? He knew it was true, yet to hear it was like a whiplash to the heart.

The man's eyes narrowed and his fingers squeezed more tightly around his sword. "He may be half ryrik, but he's also half human."

Human. The word rang in Jace's ears. No one had ever called him human. Who was this man?

The stranger turned to his horse and dug through his saddlebags. When he faced Jasper again, he had a money pouch in his hand. "I'll give you two-fifty for him."

The glint of greed flashed in Jasper's eyes. "How about three hundred?"

"I only have two-hundred fifty."

Jasper glanced past the man. "Throw in the black horse and you can have him."

Jace looked over, noticing the second horse for the first time—a stunning black stallion. Certainly he was worth far more than Jace. *Don't do it.* He almost spoke. The horse deserved far better than Jasper.

"The horse is not for sale."

Jace breathed a sigh.

"Then there's no deal," Jasper declared.

The stranger turned to his horse again, and something Jace couldn't explain sank inside him. He hadn't hoped the man would take him. He didn't possess hope anymore. But, still, it had been a chance to get away from Jasper. Whatever happened after that, he would have escaped the awful man. He prepared to watch the stranger ride away, but then the man turned back. This time he held a finely-crafted dagger along with the money pouch. He hesitated for a moment, as if reconsidering, but then he spoke.

"I'll give you this and the money."

Jasper's eyes lit up. "All right, it's a deal." He sneered at Jace. "He won't amount to anything anyway."

He snatched up the dagger and the money pouch with a wicked grin. For the ninth time, Jace had been sold. What it would mean, he could not say. The stranger seemed to be a good man, but hadn't Jace concluded there was no such thing? No doubt the man only pretended so that Jace would let his guard down—would dare to hope, only to have it crushed. Well, he wouldn't fall for it.

Jasper reached into his pocket and tossed a key into the dirt at the man's feet. The key to Jace's chains. "I wouldn't set him loose if I were you. He's likely to run off, or, even more likely, slit your throat and ride off with your goods."

Without even a parting glance, Jasper strode away. Jace glared after him, hoping never to lay eyes on the hateful man again. He then turned his gaze to his newest master.

WHEN WOULD THE act slip? When would the man's true nature show? From what Jace had experienced, there were two types of people: the cruel and the victims—the predators and the prey. This man certainly wasn't prey.

The stranger faced him and took a step closer. Jace pushed to his feet and held the man's gaze coldly. Best to show him right away who and what he was. He then eyed the man up and down. He could obviously handle himself despite his advanced years, considering the way he had taken down Jasper. Jace didn't doubt that he could wield the sword at his belt just as skillfully. A man like this wouldn't just carry it for show, the way Jasper did.

When the man spoke, his voice, though a bit rough, was calm and not harsh. "What is your name?"

Jace just stared at him. Name? No one cared about his name. He was the half-blood . . . or worse. A heavy silence hung between them. Finally, the man sighed and bent down for the key.

"Jace." He drew a breath, and the man straightened. "My name is Jace."

The man gave a slight nod. "I'm Rayad."

His perceptive eyes traveled over Jace, pausing on his wounds. Jace stiffly waited for the inspection to end. The man was probably calculating what he was actually worth and how much it would take to get him back to prime condition. Would he use him as a gladiator too? One man could make quite a profit on a fighter like Jace—even in small fights, if it involved a lot of betting. Well, he would soon find he had wasted his money. Jace didn't intend to set foot in an arena ever again. He just needed to get his hands on a blade.

At last, Rayad spoke again, the bluntness of his words shocking. "I have no notion of whether or not I can trust you. But I do want to help you and see your wounds are properly tended. I'll leave you chained until then, but when I'm done, I'll release you. After that, it's your choice. You can run or come with me. You're no longer a slave."

What? The question rang through Jace. He kept his emotions from reaching his expression, but they raced around inside of him. No longer a slave? Who was this man? Who bought a slave and then released him? It made no sense.

Rayad turned and unbuckled his sword belt, hanging it over his horse's saddle—a smart move on his part, keeping his weapons out of Jace's reach. However, Jace didn't need a weapon to be dangerous.

Gathering what appeared to be medical supplies and a full waterskin, Rayad faced Jace again. Jace eyed the waterskin, his throat aching for a drink after the exertion he had put into the fight.

"Why don't you kneel down so I can take a look at your back and other wounds?"

Jace's gaze flew to Rayad's face, instinctual warnings

shooting pain through his battered back. Kneeling was a position of submission, of cowering, of vulnerability. He never wanted to kneel before another man again.

"I have no intention of harming you." Rayad gave a dry chuckle. "Actually, I have no doubt you could outmatch me if you wanted."

Jace raised his brows slightly. Jasper would never have admitted such a thing. It was so strange. He glanced around camp. Was Jasper actually behind this? Was it some sort of cruel game? Whatever it was, the fact remained that this man had paid for him. Regardless of what he had said about Jace being free, he was still chained up. He had no choice but to obey . . . for now.

Slowly, he dropped to one knee and then the other. Rayad approached and knelt beside him. Jace could have taken him right there, but then how would he get free? He had seen the man slip the key to the chains into his saddlebags. Another wise move.

Jace tensed as Rayad lifted the back of his tunic. After a moment of silence, the man drew a deep breath. "I think this would be easier if you took your tunic off."

Reaching up with his free arm, Jace pulled his tunic over his head. The rough fabric caught along the welts, setting them aflame. He gritted his teeth in a grimace. His gaze caught Rayad's. The man had seen—seen his pain and weakness. Heat flushed through him, but the man's expression held something foreign—sympathy.

"Feeling pain isn't a weakness."

Jace looked away. Yes, it was. It was exactly that which men like Jasper and Dane preyed on.

In silence, Rayad went to work on the injuries. Jace

expected the rough treatment Jasper doled out to his injured gladiators, but Rayad took more care. Still, it hurt. Jace fought mightily to hide the pain, but he couldn't stop his breath from coming hard.

Once Rayad finished, Jace pulled his tunic back on and stood up. Now the test. Would the man turn him loose?

Rayad returned the supplies to his saddlebags and pulled out the key. He turned it in his fingers, and then glanced toward the sky. Jace had seen a few people do that before in prayer, something he knew nothing about. The few times in his younger years that he had ever cried out for help from whatever deities existed, he had received nothing but silence and more pain.

Finally, the man turned to him, and Jace lifted his chained wrist, almost daring the man to go back on his word. Taking Jace's wrist, Rayad unlocked the shackle. The chain fell at Jace's feet, and the man tossed the key away before looking him in the eyes. "You're free."

Free. He had actually done it! Jace's gaze jumped to the trees ahead. They had always called to him. He could run, hide, never be enslaved again. He then looked at the horses. Maybe he was free, but he had nothing. No food, no clothes, no money. How would he survive? Could he steal from the man who had set him free? His gaze rested again on Rayad. The man watched him and spoke calmly.

"Listen, you can go if you wish, but people would probably suspect you're a runaway, and you could be enslaved again. If you come with me, I can offer you a good, warm meal and better prepare you to go on your way."

Jace peered at him. Was it a trick? Surely there was a catch. People were *never* kind.

When he didn't speak, Rayad turned to take the horses' leads. "Why don't we head into the forest and find somewhere out of the way to set up camp for the night?" He set off for the trees.

The suspicions wouldn't leave Jace's mind, yet something also tugged at him to follow. After all, he did need food. Fine, he would go, but he would be on his guard. At the first sign that the man wasn't what he claimed to be, he would be ready to bolt. Or fight . . . if he had to.

They crossed the meadow to the forest. Jace glanced into the trees, checking the shadows for hidden threats, but kept the closest eye on Rayad. When they had gone on a good distance, Rayad left the road, cutting deeper into the forest. Jace narrowed his eyes. It was an odd move. A little heat flowed down his arms and into his fingers, and he glanced at Rayad's sword still hanging from his horse's saddle. Could he reach it if he had to?

A couple hundred yards into the forest, they reached a small clearing. Rayad stopped and looked back at Jace. "We'll camp here."

He turned to unsaddle the white horse. Jasper would never have turned his back to Jace, or any of his gladiators, without Zar there. How did he know Jace wouldn't try to kill him? He had already admitted to not knowing if he could trust Jace. Rayad was the strangest man he had ever met.

Pulling the saddle from his horse's back, the man said, "I won't force you to do anything but, if you feel up to it, you can gather some firewood while I tend the horses. Don't strain yourself—just enough to get the fire going. Then I'll start supper."

He went on with his work, and Jace stood for a moment.

Should he refuse and put to the test whether or not the man truly meant it when he said that Jace was no longer a slave? He glanced to the trees. Once he entered them, he wouldn't have to come back. With one more look at Rayad, he strode away. Slipping behind the thick undergrowth, out of view, he peered back to where Rayad was busy hobbling the horses to let them graze. He didn't seem concerned at all about Jace leaving. Jace drew his brows together, conflict warring inside of him. Could he trust this man? How would he know before it was too late? He had a chance to run. He should take it.

His stomach growled deeply, reminding him that he had nothing but the ragged, bloodstained clothes he wore. With a great sigh, Jace cast his gaze around and bent to pick up a broken tree limb. His back protested, but he had gotten used to working through pain.

Several minutes later, he returned to Rayad's camp with an armful of wood. The man looked up from where he had cleared a place for a fire, and his eyes grew just enough to let Jace know he was surprised that he had come back.

With a slight smile, Rayad pushed to his feet. "Thank you."

Jace stood dumbly. Not once in all his years had anyone ever thanked him for his service. It was simply demanded of him. He was the slave, and slaves didn't get thanks.

"Just set it down and I'll start a fire," Rayad told him.

Jace set the pile near Rayad and stepped back to watch. The fact that he didn't ask Jace to do it surprised him almost as much as the man's thank-you. Murmuring to himself, Rayad prepared rice, beans, and dried meat to heat over the fire. When it finished, he dished up a bowl and offered it to Jace. Jace took it and sat down across the fire. The scent of the food squeezed his stomach even harder in hunger. He took a bite. Though Jasper had fed his slaves better than most masters Jace had known, this simple supper tasted ten times better. At least it had some seasoning. He found himself consumed by the luxury of it, and quickly downed every bite.

Now that his stomach was contentedly full, he set the bowl aside. His gaze caught on Rayad's sword propped up next to him, and then their eyes met. The man studied him for a moment. Then he reached for the sword. Jace tensed, heat flooding his body. This was it. The man's true colors were about to show. He had known it was only a matter of time.

Rayad laid the sword on the ground between them, the hilt resting merely a foot away from Jace's hand. Jace stared at it. What was this? The man might as well have put it in his hand—a weapon—while he sat there armed with nothing more than the dagger on his belt.

"If you intend to kill me, get it over with. I won't be able to stop you, and I won't sit up all night watching you."

What was Jace to make of such words? What sort of man put his life entirely in the hands of someone like Jace when he didn't even know him? "You're not afraid?"

"Of dying? Not really." Rayad settled against his saddle. "I've lived a full life, and I'm a firm believer in King Elôm."

The fire crackled as Jace sat in silence. King Elôm. The name settled with surprising weight in Jace's mind. He had heard it once before, spoken by an old slave woman long ago. Most people cried out to Aertus and Vilai, or no god at all, but that old woman had prayed to Elôm. What sort of God was He that He gave a clearly smart man like Rayad the confidence to put his life entirely in a stranger's hands? Did

He also have something to do with why the man would pay for a slave and then free him?

"Why?" the question finally rose from Jace's growing confusion.

"Why what?"

"Why are you doing this for me—a half ryrik?" Jace grimaced. He almost choked on his next words. Hearing them in his head was one thing, but speaking them was another. Still, they were the truth. "An animal. All hate me."

He gritted his teeth and fought to swallow down the pain.

"I'm not so sure of that," Rayad said softly, shocking Jace anew. He cleared his throat. "As for your question, I don't hold with cruelty or injustice. And you may not understand, but I feel compelled to help you. It's up to you whether or not you accept my help."

Silence fell again. The man wanted to *help* Jace. He couldn't wrap his mind around it. Did he even understand the concept? People didn't help each other; at least not when they were slaves or half-blooded monsters.

He looked down at the sword and picked it up. Rayad didn't react. Jace held the weapon for a moment. The size and weight nearly matched the sword he had wielded for the last year. It felt familiar, but he hated it. Tossing the sword up into the air, he caught it by the scabbard. He met Rayad's gaze again and offered the hilt. "I won't kill you."

Jace sat and stared at the slowly dying flames of the campfire. All was quiet but the light crackle and nighttime insects. And Rayad's quiet breathing. Jace looked to where he lay on the other side of the fire. He had never truly expected the man to fall asleep. It hadn't taken long, either. He really did rest comfortably in his belief in his God.

However, Jace could not rest. Even if his body yearned for it, his mind wouldn't allow it. Today had been the strangest day of his life, and he didn't know what to do with it. He glanced at the horses standing at the rope tied between two trees. Even if he took one and rode away from here, that would still leave Rayad with a mount. That black horse stirred a longing in him to own such a fine animal.

Jace shook his head. He was already a killer; he couldn't become a thief as well. Not after what Rayad had done for him. Everything about the man said that he was telling Jace the truth—that he truly was free from slavery and free to do as he wished. But what did Jace know of freedom? What would he even do with it? People would still see him as a monster. Even free, he couldn't escape the memories that dogged him every time he closed his eyes. Those would remain to haunt and torment him for the rest of his life. Could he live with that? Flashes of his fights took over, showing him the face of each man he had killed. The guilt of their blood grew stronger with each one. Rayad may have freed him from slavery, but he would never be free of his past. He would drag it with him wherever he went.

A shudder passed through him. What kind of life was that? Why would he even *want* such a life? Maybe, if Rayad had come along years ago, before Jasper, before the fights . . . before Dane. Jace's life was marred by blood. There was no going back—no redemption. Why go forward? Even free, the guilt of his actions would torture him. He didn't think he could live with that.

Jace's heart rate increased, warming his blood. He pushed to his feet and approached Rayad silently. The man didn't stir as Jace reached out and withdrew the dagger from his belt. He stood for a moment and stared at the sleeping man, still marveling that he actually had the courage to fall asleep. Jace could kill him right here and now, without him ever knowing what happened. He squeezed the dagger. He never wanted to kill anyone again, and he had only one sure way to prevent it from happening.

Though he remained silent, in his heart he whispered a thank-you to the first man who had not treated him like an animal or monster. He then turned and crossed the small clearing, slipping into the shadows of the trees. He went on several yards before stopping. At least now Rayad would think he had simply left during the night. Jace hated that the man had spent everything he had for nothing.

Coming across an old stump, Jace sat down and looked at the dagger. He turned it in his hand so the sharp point faced him. Dim moonlight glinted along the sharp edge. He drew a long breath and let it out slowly. Around him, the nighttime bugs chirped, and frogs peeped in the distance from some far-off stream or pond. He looked at the trees again. Before today, he had only ever seen the forest from the inside of Jasper's wagon. The vastness of it always seemed to promise isolation and protection from hatred and cruelty.

Not from his past, however. He couldn't hide from that. He tightened his fingers around the dagger and raised it to chest height.

For a long moment, he sat frozen. With one thrust, this whole cruel life could end. It was as simple as that . . . yet something stayed his hand. Like an ember fighting for life, sparks of hope floated among the cries to give up—hope that, just maybe, somehow there could be a life beyond the pain—that, if he held on just a little longer, he would find it. That he could somehow leave his past behind. The desperation for such a thing left a tight ache in his chest.

He glanced back toward Rayad's camp. Could the man help him find such a life? Would he be willing once he learned what Jace truly was? Would he turn on him and see him as a monster like everyone else?

He shook his head. Hope was dangerous. It seemed only to exist to be crushed. He couldn't take that chance. To try and then fail would be unbearable. The guilt alone gnawed too deeply for him to believe he could ever escape it.

He gripped the dagger until his hand shook . . . but he couldn't go through with it. With a cry, he threw it to the ground. Why couldn't he do it? Was it his accursed ryrik blood again, fighting for survival? After everything he had been through, he could finally take his life into his own hands and decide what to do with it—decide to put an end to the misery. Yet that was just it. He had control for the first time in his life. How could he not discover what such freedom was—not rise above the misery and fight to *live*?

Pushing to his feet, Jace walked to the dagger and picked it up. He was probably making a mistake. The people of Ilyon would still fear and hate him. He still had the blood of many men on his hands, but some fighting force inside him would not be denied. Whether it was a stubborn hope or his ryrik blood, he had to give this life a chance. He had fought so hard for so long. He couldn't just surrender now.

Breathing out heavily, Jace walked back to camp. Rayad still slept, unaware of his struggle, and Jace returned his dagger.

He went back to his place on the other side of the fire and grabbed the blanket. Rolling up inside it, he looked up at the stars, and then closed his eyes, letting his body claim the sleep it so craved.

JACE JERKED AWAKE, his heart ricocheting against his ribs. Murky images from his dreams still claimed his mind. Where was he? He looked around, blinking. Trees. The clearing. He breathed out as everything from the day before settled and the dark dreams faded.

"Sleep well?"

He looked up at Rayad, whose cheerful, rested expression still left him confused. Would he ever get used to such questions?

"Yes," he murmured at last. Once he had drifted off, he'd slept deeply . . . until the dreams.

"Good. When we've eaten, we can be on our way." Rayad paused. "That is, if you'd like to join me."

"Where are you going?"

"I have some old friends who live a few days north of here near Kinnim. I hope to stay with them for a time until other arrangements can be made."

Jace frowned. "You have no home?"

Something changed in Rayad's expression, a sadness settling in his eyes. "No, not anymore . . . I'm on the run."

Now Jace raised his brows. The man was a fugitive? All sorts of possibilities ran through his mind, but he didn't have a chance to contemplate them before Rayad answered his unspoken questions.

"I'm wanted by the emperor's men. They want me for speaking out against his desire to force Arcacia to worship his false gods . . ."

As far as Jace knew, the emperor worshiped Aertus and Vilai. He had never heard anyone call them false gods before. Not that it meant anything to him which gods existed and which ones didn't, or who Rayad chose to believe in.

"They consider me a rebel . . . among other things," Rayad continued. "What about you? Is there someplace you'd rather go?"

An unexpected pain tore through Jace's heart, almost making him wince. Seventeen years old, and he didn't have a single place that he could even remotely call home. He turned his face away and shook his head.

Rayad was silent for a moment and turned to his pack. He pulled out some food from his pack and handed it to Jace. Jace said nothing, but his stomach growled. Fights always increased his appetite, once his stomach settled.

"My friends," Rayad went on, "they're an older couple."

Jace glanced up, not sure how much older they could be, since the man wasn't young himself.

Rayad smirked at him. "Yes, older than me, and very kind. They live on a small farm about ten miles from the nearest village, so there won't be many people, and no one to come looking for us. So, would you like to join me?"

Jace swallowed a bite of jerky, though it went down harder than it should have. The idea of a secluded farm filled his heart with a yearning he hadn't known before. Could it truly be real? He didn't even know this couple Rayad referred to. More importantly, they didn't know *him*. "I don't think your friends would have me." His voice dropped lower. "I'm a killer."

"I don't believe that."

Rayad's reply startled him, but he didn't truly know Jace either. He didn't know Jace's past—the things he had done. He should tell him, but spilling the dark secrets scared him even more than entering the arena.

"I know Kalli and Aldor will welcome you," Rayad spoke with confidence. "Trust me, you'll never meet kinder or gentler souls."

Jace sighed and gave a slow nod. At least he could try it. He glanced at the knife he had taken last night. He would always have a plan, an escape, if things didn't work out . . . if he couldn't live with himself.

They ate their brief breakfast in silence, and then Rayad rose and saddled his white horse. When he went to get the stallion, the black horse pranced around and tried to yank out of his grip.

"Oh, don't you start with me," Rayad grumbled and tugged at the lead. "Come on."

The stallion planted his feet and would not budge. Jace eyed the stubborn animal, drawn to it.

"Well, if you aren't the most stubborn, ornery . . ." Rayad flicked the end of the rope at the horse's hindquarters. The horse jumped sideways, but still refused to move.

Jace could no longer resist. He pushed to his feet and approached Rayad. "Can I try?"

Rayad gave him a surprised look. He hesitated a moment,

but then handed over the lead. "Just don't let him go, or it'll take us all morning to catch him. And beware. He's never liked strangers."

Jace had worked with many so-called unruly horses. All they took was bit of time and understanding. "What's his name?"

"Niton."

Jace repeated the name. It suited the horse.

Niton's ears pricked forward as he focused on Jace. He blew loudly a couple of times, before his breathing quieted. Jace waited until the stallion calmed, and then he approached slowly.

"Easy, boy," he murmured. When he reached Niton, he ran a gentle hand down the horse's neck and shoulders. Niton stood alert, but perfectly still. With gentle pressure on the rope, Jace led the horse toward Rayad.

The man stared open-mouthed at him. "How did you do that?"

Jace shrugged. He had always felt a connection with animals; more so than with people. One of his masters said it was his ryrik blood, since they were animals too. "I've worked with horses before. I like them." He ran his hand down Niton's face and looked into one of his dark eyes. "They don't know what I am."

For a silent moment, Rayad just kept staring at him. Jace tensed. Was the man starting to realize just what an oddity Jace was? Would he regret buying his freedom? Would he take it back and sell him first chance he got? Fear twisted Jace's gut.

Finally, Rayad turned. "We best get moving. Aros can bear both of us."

"Can I ride Niton?" The question left Jace's mouth before he had a chance to think it over. It seemed a practical choice, but he never would have been so bold as to ask Jasper such a thing. For all Rayad knew, he could just ride off with Niton.

Rayad stopped and turned again. His voice flat, he said, "Niton's never had a man on his back, and the way things are going, I doubt he ever will."

Jace arched one of his eyebrows. This man had no idea how many wild horses he had tamed. He could ride Niton. He had no doubt about that.

Rayad blew out a sigh as he held Jace's unwavering gaze. "All right, it's your body."

Jace almost laughed. He had taken far worse beatings from people than he ever had from working with a horse.

"But like I said," Rayad warned, "don't let him go . . . if you can help it."

He was actually going to let him ride the horse. A smile rose, unbidden. It felt so strange. Only Rohir and Strune had been able to make him smile, but, even then, it took a lot. His heart rate accelerating, Jace tossed the end of the lead rope over Niton's neck and tied it to his halter. Stepping to the stallion's side, he took the makeshift reins and a handful of Niton's thick mane in his hand. With a deep breath, he jumped up and swung himself up onto the horse's back.

Niton's muscles rippled beneath him, and the horse pranced around and tossed his head. Jace gripped with his legs as the horse stepped back skittishly and then reared. When Niton's front hooves hit the ground again, Jace laid the reins across his neck. The horse hesitated at first, but then turned in a circle, first to the right and then the left. Once settled into following the commands, Jace brought him to a halt.

Patting the horse's neck, he looked down at Rayad, who was staring again. Jace couldn't help smirking slightly. He liked to prove people wrong.

Rayad shook his head. "You have quite a talent, Jace."

He turned for his other horse. Once he mounted, they set off in the direction of the road. Jace moved Niton up beside Rayad, for a moment completely reveling in the feeling of being able to ride. His previous masters had never let him do any riding outside of a corral. However, when they reached the road and turned north, his nerves took over again, robbing him of the joy he found in the ride. What would he find at the end of this journey? Rayad had told him where they were going, but would it be as he described?

With a jolt, Jace sat upright, gasping for breath. Heat burned through his muscles as phantom images of death and violence still swirled about him. His heart threatened to burst with its racing. He gulped in a cool breath of air and tried to calm it as he brushed away the hair clinging to his sweaty face. Though the nightmare's images faded from his mind, their disturbing touch lingered.

"Are you all right?"

Jace flinched and looked over at Rayad. Even in full darkness he could see him as if twilight had just fallen. He appeared genuinely concerned, but Jace looked away, heat now prickling up his scalp. "I'm fine."

A silence followed, but then Rayad rustled around in his bedroll. "Might as well get up. It's almost dawn. If we get an early start, we won't reach the farm so late."

Jace glanced at him again as the man rolled up his blankets and then turned to stoke the embers of the fire. A few days had passed since they had set out on their journey. While they didn't talk a lot, Rayad did try to engage him in conversation, something no one else had ever done. He had even traded some of his meager supplies to get Jace a new shirt in the small village they had passed along the way. All of his actions said he was a man of honor, but the closer they came to reaching the farm, the more Jace's anxieties grew. What if it was all just a ruse—a way to make him trust Rayad and go along with him until they reached somewhere he would have friends who could help him control Jace? Every night before Jace fell asleep, he lay awake and wondered if this was a mistake—if he should have just ended it that first night. The fear of potentially finding out he had been tricked was almost too much.

Shoving to his feet, he walked over to Niton. The feel of the animal's strong neck and warm coat against his palms calmed him—just like Rohir had done. He ran his hands slowly over the horse, breathing deeply as the last of the heat in his veins died away. Though the fears remained, he must go on. He had to know the truth.

In a few minutes, Rayad had the fire going enough to heat some coffee, and Jace joined him. Coffee was a new experience for him. At first, he had found it so bitter he couldn't imagine why anyone would willingly drink it, but, after a couple more cups, he had begun to enjoy it. They sat in silence for a moment, sipping the hot liquid and eating their breakfast. Though he stared into the fire, Jace felt Rayad watching him. The man had seen him dreaming the other nights too. Jace hated how weak it made him feel, but the horrible dreams of death and pain wouldn't let up. Ever since Jasper had killed Strune, they plagued him almost nightly.

"Are you a follower of Aertus and Vilai?"

Jace's attention snapped to Rayad. The man peered at him curiously.

"No."

Rayad nodded slowly. "What about King Elôm? Have you heard of Him?"

Jace looked down into his nearly-empty coffee cup before meeting Rayad's gaze again. "Once . . . I heard a woman pray to Him." He straightened his shoulders. "But no god cares about someone like me."

He waited for Rayad to disagree. Instead, he asked, "Why do you think that?"

Jace scrunched his forehead. It was obvious. "I'm half ryrik. I have no soul."

Rayad looked him in the eyes in a probing, yet understanding, way. "And who told you that?"

Jace gritted his teeth. Why did he want him to answer such questions? It was hard enough to know he had no soul, why did he have to speak of it? "No one had to tell me. Everyone knows ryriks are soulless."

"But you're only half ryrik," Rayad said quietly.

Jace shook his head, that terrifying heat rising in his blood, as if to prove his next words. "Half or not, I still have their blood. That makes me no better than one of them."

His chest grew tight, his limbs flushing with warmth, and his eyes stung. Blinking hard, he tossed away the rest of his coffee and turned to roll up his blanket. He had to do something with his hands. Something non-violent. The man didn't understand. Jace was an animal, pure and simple. Why speak of it if it wouldn't change anything? All it did was cause pain. Maybe that's what Rayad wanted . . . He dug his fingers into his blanket.

"I know Elôm well, or at least as well as a mortal can after a lifetime of faith, and I believe He cares deeply for you."

Jace stilled at Rayad's words. A God who cared for him? Impossible. He was a half-ryrik monster with no soul. Even if he did have a soul, what kind of God would care about a killer?

"Perhaps," Rayad continued slowly, "you'll let me tell you about Him sometime."

Jace did not answer. He didn't believe it—*couldn't* believe it. In the end, reality would only crush him. However, some tugging inside of him wanted to hear—wanted it to be true.

"THE FARM SHOULD be just over the rise," Rayad announced.

Jace set his gaze on the path ahead, where the trees thinned out. The long shadows of evening crisscrossed the trail before them. They had left the main road some time ago. It didn't appear that people came this way often, a good indication that Rayad had told him the truth. Even so, Jace's heart rattled with the unease that had grown steadily throughout the day. What would Kalli and Aldor be like? What if they didn't accept him the way Rayad assured him they would? What if they immediately noticed the signs of his ryrik blood and threw him out? His stomach churned with the unanswered questions. How could he dare hope to find welcome here, when he had never found it anywhere else in all his seventeen years?

When they crested the rise, Jace drew Niton to a halt. Up ahead in a small, bowl-like valley rested a farm. Lush crops grew in the fields around a barn, where cows, sheep, and a couple of draft horses grazed in their pasture. To the left of the barn were the farmyard and a large cabin, in which the windows glowed with beckoning candlelight. Jace's breath caught. It looked so peaceful and . . . home-like. Could it possibly offer what its appearance promised?

"We should be right in time for supper," Rayad said, snapping Jace from his thoughts. The man smiled encouragingly at him. "Kalli is one of the best cooks I know."

He continued on, down into the little valley. Jace held back a moment, gathering his nerve. If he could walk into an arena and face death, surely he could do this. But, somehow, he would rather have his foe visible and standing in front of him. The unknown and the uncertainties proved much more formidable than any flesh-and-blood opponent. With a hard breath, he followed Rayad.

As they rode into the farmyard, the smell of animals mixed with the warm dewy air reminded him of the country estates he had belonged to before Jasper. Yet he saw no slaves or slave quarters. He heard no rattling chains or cracking whips—only a peaceful and alluring evening quiet.

They stopped at the cabin, and Rayad slid down first. Jace followed more slowly, a flight response trying to take hold of him. He wasn't ready for reality to mar the scene around him—a scene too perfect to be real, but one that stirred the yearning inside him.

They tied the horses to the porch railing. As Rayad approached the steps, the cabin door opened, spilling light out onto the porch, and a figure stepped out. Jace shrank deeper into the shadows at Niton's side and observed a man of about seventy with snowy white hair and a beard. Despite his age, he looked strong—strong enough to work the land around the cabin.

"Looking for a place to put up for the night, traveler?" the man questioned with a welcoming curiosity.

"More than just the night, I hope," Rayad replied, a smile in his voice.

He climbed the stairs to the porch. Once the man got a good look at him in the light, a wide grin split his face. "Rayad!" He turned to look back into the cabin. "Kalli, it's Rayad!"

An exclamation came from inside and, with a bustle of movement, a woman around Aldor's age appeared. She was shorter than her husband, and her plump figure filled out her homespun dress.

"Bless the King! It is so good to see you!" She drew Rayad into an eager embrace.

Rayad chuckled and patted her back lightly. "It is good to see you too."

Such a show of affection was foreign to Jace. Was this normal amongst free people? He had to resist as the urge to hide escalated its assault. It overwhelmed him how little he knew of life beyond slavery. How could he even hope to navigate it?

Rayad stepped back from Kalli and clasped Aldor's arm in a hearty grip. "It's been far too long."

"That it has," Aldor agreed. "I hope things have been well with you."

A tired look crossed Rayad's face. "Well, I'm alive. That's more than enough to praise Elôm for, but I am looking for a place to stay for a while."

"You know you're more than welcome here."

Aldor gestured to usher Rayad inside, but Rayad paused. "I brought a friend with me."

He turned and motioned to Jace, who stood frozen for a moment. The strangeness of being called a friend threw him off, but it was the fear of rejection that fueled his hesitation. Forcing his body to obey, he stepped forward and climbed the steps with heavy feet. He met Aldor's eyes briefly, but could not hold them. Rayad rested a hand on his shoulder. Jace flinched at the touch, but then found it surprisingly reassuring.

"This is Jace. He traveled north with me from Troas."

A brief silence followed; just long enough to let Jace know the couple studied him. He struggled not to squirm. Would they know right away what he was? Would they allow him into their home?

Then Kalli spoke, her voice just as warm and welcoming as before. "Please, do come in. I was just putting supper on the table."

Rayad followed the couple inside, and Jace stepped in behind him. The savory scent of beef and steamed vegetables hit him immediately and set his mouth to watering. Such scents had filled the kitchen where he had once worked. He made a quick scan of the cabin interior in search of any weapons or threats, something he had learned to do with every new place he entered. Aside from an old sword gathering dust in the corner and an unstrung bow, the place appeared harmless. In fact, it looked set up for comfort. To the left was a living area with comfortable seating, while the right contained a dining table and cabinets full of cookware and baking supplies. A fire crackled in a large fireplace, adding its light to that of the candles.

"I hope it isn't too much trouble that we showed up unannounced," Rayad said.

"Not at all! There is plenty." Kalli's skirts swished the plank floor as she whisked toward the table. "Just let me set places for you."

As she gathered more plates and utensils, Aldor turned to Rayad. "Do you want me to take care of your horses for you?"

"They'll be all right while we eat. Jace and I can help you once we've finished."

Aldor nodded, and they went to the table. Kalli motioned Jace to one of the extra chairs, and he slowly took a seat. He'd never eaten at a table. He wasn't even sure of the proper way to do so. He glanced helplessly at Rayad. Hopefully, imitating him would be enough. Before any food was served, his three dining companions bowed their heads, and Aldor said a prayer to Elôm. Jace had seen Rayad do the same before meals on the trail, though he had prayed silently. Jace shifted in his chair. While he didn't think he could ever believe the way these people did, he hated being an outsider.

When the brief prayer ended, they passed the food around the table. Jace discreetly watched Rayad fill his plate as each dish came to him and did the same. The mouthwatering aroma of the food tempted him mightily to dive in, but he forced himself to wait until Rayad took his first bite. Taking up a fork, Jace tore a piece of beef from the thick slice on his plate and stuck it in his mouth. The warm juices, infused with salt and spices, ignited his taste buds. Until this moment, he hadn't known the true taste of meat. Its savory tenderness was unlike anything he had ever eaten. He speared a couple of carrots next, which were steamed and dripping in melted butter. At first, the food was all he could focus on, overwhelmed by tastes he hadn't known existed, but slowly he became aware of the conversation around the table.

"We didn't have much choice but to leave," Rayad was saying. "They would have either killed us outright or brought us back to the fort and executed us. You're as close to family as I have besides Warin, so I thought I'd come here."

"Well, I'm glad you did," Kalli replied, her wrinkled face sympathetic. "Those of us who follow the King need to stick together these days."

Aldor nodded in agreement. "Especially if things get worse, which I'm afraid they will."

"I fear so too," Rayad replied. "The emperor is up to something. He can't hide his hatred of us forever."

After that, the conversation lightened as Rayad asked about the farm. As far as Jace could tell, he hadn't said anything about how the two of them had met or where Jace had come from. At every lull in the conversation, he held his breath, waiting for it to come out. He knew Rayad couldn't keep his secrets, but Jace dreaded how the couple might react to him in their home once they knew.

Shortly after supper was finished, Jace followed Rayad and Aldor outside to take care of the horses. By this time, stars sprinkled the sky, and one of the two moons was visible over the trees. They gave the horses some hay and a quick brushing before returning to the cabin. Kalli had the table cleared, and she turned to them as they entered. "I just put a kettle on for tea, if you would like some."

The men resumed their previous seats at the table. Now that he didn't have anything to eat, Jace wasn't sure what to do. He would rather have stayed out in the barn with Niton. He'd been tempted to ask, but what kind of impression would that have made?

Rayad and Aldor conversed easily, yet, even after the days spent with Rayad, Jace didn't have enough practice to join in. After all, what would he talk about? Certainly nothing befitting polite conversation.

A moment later, Kalli rounded the table and set a plate near him. "I didn't make anything fancy for dessert, seeing as how I didn't know we'd have company, but here are some shortbread cookies I made earlier."

Jace stared at the sugary, golden-brown squares. Slaves *never* had such delicacies. Even though Rayad had freed him, it just didn't seem . . . right.

"Go ahead, dear, take some," Kalli urged. She chuckled. "If you don't, Aldor will end up eating them all."

The older man laughed. "That's true. You'd better take some."

How could Jace refuse? He reached for one of the cookies and took a bite. The buttery sweetness of it melted on his tongue and tasted every bit as heavenly as he had dreamed such things would taste. Swallowing the first bite, he glanced up at Kalli and murmured, "Thank you."

Her smile crinkled her eyes and filled Jace's chest with comfortable warmth. "Have as many as you want."

Taking another bite, Jace savored every crumb.

When the kettle boiled, Kalli served them each a small cup of berry tea, but did not join them at the table.

"I'll go upstairs and prepare your rooms," she told Rayad. "It's been ages since we've had any guests staying with us."

"Do you want help?" Aldor asked.

"No, no, you stay and keep them company. I'll only be a bit."

She disappeared through a door at the far side of the room before reappearing a minute later with a bundle of blankets. After collecting a bucket of water, she climbed a log staircase up to the second floor.

"It will be nice to have you around." Aldor smiled at Rayad. "We don't get to town much these days, so we don't see many people."

From here, they went on to talk of the nearest town of Kinnim. Jace didn't listen very closely. He had no interest in towns or ever setting foot in one again. Instead, his gaze settled on the cookies still sitting before him. He had never been able to take what he wanted; only what he was given. His body rebelled at the thought of taking another, but, eventually, he could no longer resist the lingering taste in his mouth. He took another cookie from the plate and bit into it.

He had just allowed himself to take a third when Kalli returned.

"My!" she said, winded. "I didn't realize how much dust and cobwebs had collected up there. I took care of the worst of it, but it could use a proper cleaning. The beds have clean linens, though, and I filled the pitchers with fresh water."

"That will be perfect," Rayad told her. "I could sleep in the barn and still be perfectly happy."

Kalli moved along the table and smiled at Jace. "I see you're enjoying those cookies."

His cheeks flushed, but her smile was so kind, his embarrassment faded. "Yes."

"Good. I will have to make more." She joined them at the table, and quickly fell into conversation with the other men.

Thankfully, no questions were directed Jace's way. They seemed to understand that he didn't wish to share his story. At least not right now. Once he did, all of this would probably end.

About an hour later, Kalli's gentle gaze fell on him. "It's getting quite late. Would you like me to show you to your room? Then you can decide if you feel like turning in or not."

Jace nodded. He wasn't tired, not really, but a need to be alone had grown inside him. As kind as Kalli and Aldor were to him, he needed seclusion to think and process the evening.

Kalli rose from the table, and Jace followed her. Upstairs, she led him down a short hall and into a small room. A bed rested near the room's one window, with a dresser off to the side. Jace just stood a moment, awe gripping him. He'd never slept in a real bed or had a room to himself. He almost shrank away from Kalli, undeserving of such luxury.

"As I said, there's water in the pitcher." Kalli gestured to the white porcelain pitcher and washbasin on the dresser, completely missing Jace's hesitation. He tried to swallow it down as she turned to him and handed him the candle she carried. "If you need anything else, just ask."

Jace nodded, and another thank-you came out as little more than a whisper. Her smile seemed to touch his heart with a gentle hand, and then she left him alone, pulling the door closed behind her. Jace stood still and stared at it for a long time. He breathed hard, his chest weighted. For days, he hadn't allowed himself to believe things were really as Rayad had described, but, now that he was here, he saw that Rayad, Aldor, and Kalli were good people—*truly* good people . . . too good to bestow such kindness on someone like him.

Slowly, he turned and crossed the room, setting the candle on the dresser. Then he walked to the bed. He looked at it for a moment before sinking down onto the edge. The mattress gave way comfortably beneath him, and he ran his hand along the soft quilt. Crickets chirped outside, the sound drifting through the partially open window. It mingled with the hum of voices coming through the floorboards from below.

As Jace sat and listened, a fearful curiosity overcame him. Was Rayad telling them? His heart jumped into his throat. He pushed up from the bed and silently crossed the room. At the door, he reached for the knob, but paused. They had to know. If he stayed here, they would have to know what sort of man they sheltered. They deserved that knowledge. It wouldn't be right to make any sort of decision without it. They also had every right to ask him to leave once they knew. The thought ripped into his heart like a whip.

He squeezed his eyes shut. They would make him leave. They were far too kind and too gentle to have a dangerous half-ryrik in their home. His shoulders sagged. He just had to accept it.

Unable to bear hearing the conversation below, he returned to the bed. He pulled off his clothes, dirtied from travel, and crawled under the covers. For tonight, he would try to pretend he belonged and actually had a life here. Once it ended, the chance would probably never come again.

A ROOSTER CROWED, jolting Jace awake. For a moment, he thought he was in his cell under Jasper's house, but one look around the room reminded him where he was. It also brought back all the turmoil that had surrounded him until he had finally drifted off. He let out a deep sigh and rubbed his hands over his face. At least he hadn't dreamt last night. He had slept far too well for that. However, as comfortable as the bed was, his anxiety wouldn't let him stay still. Pushing back the quilt, he got out of bed and dressed. He glanced out the window. The sun barely peeked over the trees.

Quietly, he left the room, hoping Rayad would be up, but his door was closed. Jace hesitated. No voices came from downstairs. Maybe he could slip outside to look around without anyone knowing. He crept down the stairs. When he neared the bottom, a cheerful humming reached his ears. He halted and peered toward the kitchen. Kalli stood near the fireplace, working on breakfast. He glanced back up the stairs, about to retreat to his room, but then she turned and spotted him. Her face lit up in a smile. "Good morning, dear."

Jace stood at a loss. Surely Rayad told them about his mixed blood and gladiator past last night when they were alone, but Kalli's smile hadn't changed. He echoed her and stepped awkwardly down the remaining steps. Now what?

Kalli returned to stirring whatever batter she was working on, but she cast another glance his way. "Rayad said you like horses."

Jace nodded and slowly approached the table.

"If you'd like, you can go out to the barn. Aldor's out there. I know he'd love to show you Bell and Button."

Jace frowned.

Kalli caught his expression and chuckled. "They're his two roan plow horses. Treats them like a pair of puppies."

Jace's expression cleared. A man who gave his plow horses such names clearly cared for them, unlike some men Jace had known. He glanced toward the door. He would like to see the horses, but he held back. The turmoil of last night would not let him go. Not until he had answers. Though he hated to admit it, he was terrified. Still, he had to know. Gathering his courage, he stopped at the end of the table across from Kalli and gripped the back of one of the chairs.

"Did Rayad tell you?"

She paused and looked up at him. Her expression grew serious, and Jace's stomach clenched. This was it.

"Yes, he did."

Jace nodded slowly, hanging his head. His throat swelled, but he forced himself to speak. "I'll leave, then."

He could hardly bear the brief moment of silence that seemed to stretch for an eternity, but then Kalli spoke.

"I'd be rather disappointed if you did."

Jace's head shot up, and he met her gaze. She was serious. "How could you want me to stay, now that . . ." He swallowed hard. "Now that you know what I am?"

Kalli went back to working, but her voice was thoughtful. "Well, it's just been me and Aldor here for years. It would be nice to have a young person around again."

Jace shook his head. How could she be so calm? The fearful, loathing whispers and murmurs he had heard his whole life echoed inside him. That was how people normally reacted. Not with such composure as Kalli possessed.

"But I'm . . . half ryrik. I've . . . done things . . ." He grimaced.

Kalli looked up at him again. "Yes . . . but I don't believe having a certain type of blood decides what type of person you are. As for what you've done . . . that is now the past. Your future doesn't have to be the same."

Jace stared at her. Did she fully understand? "How do you know you can trust me?"

"I don't," Kalli said quietly, "but I do trust Elôm, and I think He brought you here for a reason."

Jace stood speechless. He had seen the height of bravado and apparent fearlessness from the men he had faced in the arenas and the gladiators he had trained beside, but none of them came close to sharing the strength he sensed in this old woman. To know what he was and to stand completely undaunted . . . where did such courage come from?

After a long, silent moment, a hint of a smile sparkled in her eyes. "Why don't you go on out to the barn and have a look around? Aldor will let you know when breakfast is ready."

Unable to do anything else, Jace turned for the door and let himself outside numbly. He couldn't wrap his mind around what had just happened. Was it even real? Would he wake up to find that even his dreams played cruel tricks on him, giving him the first real hope he had ever known, only to dash it as soon as he awakened?

Before he knew it, he stood at the open barn door. Aldor's voice came from inside.

"Now, now, Trudy, let's not have any of that. You just let me finish up and then you can go back out to your grazing." A low moo came, almost as if in answer, and Aldor chuckled. "Yes, yes, I'll be quick about it. Don't get impatient."

Jace stepped hesitantly into the barn, drawn by curiosity. He found Aldor sitting on a small stool, milking one of the cows from the pasture. The cow flicked her golden-brown tail, catching Aldor in the back of the head.

"Trudy," he scolded gently, "didn't I just tell you I was almost finished?"

Before he could stop himself, a quiet laugh rose up Jace's throat. The only person he had ever known to talk to animals like that was himself, and that was only because he had no one else.

Aldor looked up. Jace's mirth vanished, afraid he would be upset, but the man grinned. "Jace! A lovely morning, isn't it?"

Jace dug his nails into his palm. The pain wasn't that of his dreams. This must be real. He nodded, though he hadn't even noticed the weather. "Yes." He cleared his throat. It was so strange trying to converse normally. "Um, Kalli said something about you showing me Bell and Button." Just saying the names eased a little of his tension.

Still smiling, Aldor nodded. "Sure thing. Just let me finish up with old Trudy here."

While Aldor milked the cow, Jace turned and walked to Niton's stall. The stallion pawed at the ground, as if anxious to get outside. Jace didn't blame him.

"Morning, boy." He stroked the horse's neck.

Niton quieted and nuzzled Jace's shoulder, drawing a smile from him.

As soon as Aldor finished, he led Jace out to one of the pastures, where two large roan horses grazed. When the pair spotted them, they both trotted to meet them. A corner of Jace's lips lifted again as he recalled how Kalli had said her husband treated the horses. They almost did resemble two giant puppies with their eager approach. While they weren't as sleek and impressive-looking as Niton, Jace still enjoyed being around them. They certainly were powerful animals, but very gentle as they nosed him curiously. Aldor told him all about how they were twins that he had raised and trained himself. Though Jace struggled, stilted by awkwardness at first, Aldor quickly put him at ease. Sharing a love for horses and other animals allowed Jace to speak with the man more easily than he did with most people.

Sometime later, Aldor looked toward the cabin. "Mmm, I don't know about you, but I think I smell Kalli's pancakes."

A delicious scent did seem to drift in the fresh air.

"Let's go have breakfast," Aldor said.

Jace followed him to the barn, where he helped carry one of the milk pails. In the yard between the barn and the cabin, he paused, the realness of this place hitting him. He looked around the little valley, and a word settled in his mind—*home.* Could this be it? Could this really be a home for him? Kalli's words echoed in his mind, as if someone were sending a gentle reminder. *I do trust Elôm, and I think He brought you here for a reason.* Rayad had said he believed Elôm cared for Jace. Did He do this?

It seemed so impossible that a God would take any time to care or even notice someone like Jace—someone so unworthy. Yet this place was real. Against everything he had come to believe about the world, here was a place of shelter and kindness, and, for the first time in his life, his future didn't look so bleak. Instead, like a bright light in the darkness he had known for so long, there was hope.

True hope.

JACE'S STORY CONTINUES IN...

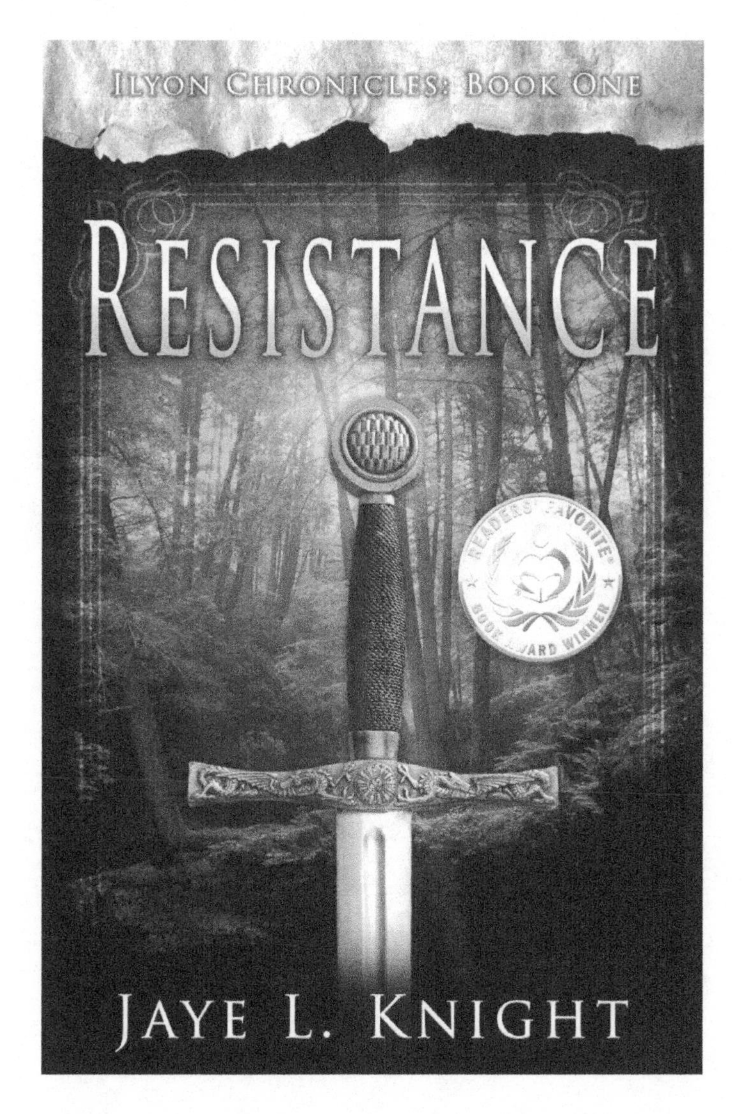

Want to discuss what you just read with other readers?
Visit: **www.jayelknight.boards.net**

For more "behind the scenes" information on Ilyon Chronicles, visit: **www.ilyonchronicles.blogspot.com**

To see Jaye's inspiration boards and character "casting" visit: **www.pinterest.com/jayelknight**

ACKNOWLEDGEMENTS

I want to give a huge thank you to the growing community of readers who are taking part in this adventure with me. Your overwhelming support is what every author dreams of having.

And special thanks goes to Grace Gidman for the name Strune. The moment I saw your suggestions on Facebook, that name stood out to me.

About the Author

Jaye L. Knight is an award-winning author, homeschool graduate, and shameless tea addict with a passion for Christian fantasy. Armed with an active imagination and love for adventure, Jaye weaves stories of truth, faith, and courage with the message that even in the deepest darkness, God's love shines as a light to offer hope. She has been penning stories since the age of eight and resides in the Northwoods of Wisconsin.

To learn more about Jaye and her work, visit:
www.jayelknight.com